MOTIVATION

MASTERING THE GAME

a novel by

SWIFT

Copyright © 2014 Swift

Published by:

R H Publishing, LLC
P.O.Box11642
Milwaukee, WI 53211
www.swiftnovels.com

Visit our website @ www.swiftnovels.com

ISBN 13: 978-0615834696
ISBN 10: 0615834698
LCCN: 2014915176

Cover designed by No Nonsense Enterprise
Cover photo by Mike's Photoshop @ 414-617-5924
Cover model Heavy

MOTIVATION
MASTERING THE GAME

Glenn and Mario "Keep Ya' Head
Up!! It won't be long..."

Chapter 1

The skies where calm as the plane floated through the air. They had been traveling for about an hour and a half now and all the passengers on the United Airlines flight where pretty relaxed and quiet, except for a baby heard crying and a Japanese couple talking and laughing amongst themselves in their native tongue. The stewardess walked down the aisle for her last round of catering to the passengers as the captain announced on the intercom that the flight was on schedule and they should be arriving in Milwaukee, Wisconsin within the next forty-five minutes.

Keyshawn Watson was asleep; tired from a long day and night of packing and preparing himself for his trip back home. It had been two years since he had been in Milwaukee. He was sent to live with his grandmother in McComb, Mississippi by his mother, due to his constant juvenile delinquency and his run-ins with police back home. He was suddenly awaking by the laughter that was growing louder from the Japanese couple who were seated just across the aisle from him one row up. The attendant was at his seat now as he was staring out the window looking at what appeared to be the St. Louis Arch.

"Hi Ma'am, would you like me to throw your trash away and do you need anything else?" she was speaking to an older Caucasian woman who was seated in the aisle seat next to Keyshawn.

"Yes, here you are and I won't be needing anything else, thank you, young lady."

"And what about you sir, would you like to throw that away?" the attendant was referring to the empty soda can that Keyshawn had in the cup holder of the seat.

"Yes," he said as he handed the can to her. "I don't need anything else, but can you tell me how long it'll be before we get to Milwaukee."

"Yes, the captain announced a few minutes ago that it'll be about forty-five minutes," she said.

"Okay thank you," he said before reaching a small carryon bag to find his walkman. He put on the headset and pressed play as he began listening to the latest CD that he had bought the day before he left McComb. It was Coo Coo Cal's newest joint, "My Projects." Keyshawn had seen him on *Rap City* in the basement and when he discovered that the rapper was from Milwaukee, he had to represent. As he listened, he began to think of home. Keyshawn missed the Mil (as the locals referred to it). He thought about his mom and his twin, Keysha; both of them were the most important women in his life. He hadn't seen them since last Christmas when they came to McComb to spend the holidays with him and the family.

Keyshawn and his sister moved to Milwaukee with their mother Michelle when they were two years old. They lived with Michelle's aunt for about six months, until Michelle was able to secure a job at A.O. Smith, a local steel factory in Milwaukee. Once she was able to save up enough money, they moved into an upper duplex on 11th and Capitol Drive, it was a nice working-class neighborhood where everybody looked out for one another. The twins shared a bedroom there until they were around ten years old, at which time they had moved a couples of blocks away into a larger house that their mother was able to buy from hard work and her savings from A.O. Smith.

It was a nice brick home facing Capitol Drive, a single family unit with three bedrooms, a remodeled basement, and a beautiful yard out back. Since they had a ping pong table in the basement that was where Keyshawn spent most his afternoons when he got out of school. Keysha would be upstairs watching TV or at the local library. She had a profound love for reading. Their mother, Michelle, worked a lot of overtime; she wanted to do her best for the kids. Keyshawn made many friends in the neighborhood, all the kids who heard about the ping pong table would want to come over and play the game with him. They also enjoyed playing on the concrete slab in the back of their garage. But the more Keyshawn mixed with the kids in the neighborhood, the more he started to venture out into the community. Particularly south of where he lived because his mother forbid them to cross Capitol Drive, she also instructed him not to venture too far south near a street called Atkinson; the people on this end of the neighborhood weren't your typical everyday citizens. This part of the vicinity was the actual "hood" where everything that could happen, will happen eventually.

But boys will be boys, and Keyshawn was no exception. He quickly grew tired of the acquaintances he had made and found himself drifting more toward the kids near Atkinson. One in particular was Devin, but everybody called him Red because of his light skin and freckles. Keyshawn and Red first met at the corner store everybody went to in the hood called Starks. They were both in line waiting to pay for their snacks when Red started talking to him.

"Aye, you just move around here or something?" he said, not recognizing him from the regular kids that he usually saw in the hood.

Keyshawn's first thought was to say yeah, but he quickly changed his mind from fear of being viewed as a possible victim.

"No, I been over here."

"Then why I don't know you? I know everybody around here, I think you lying," Red said.

"I used to stay on 11th, now I stay down the street," Keyshawn replied.

"Oh, so that's why you paying for all that stuff," Red said as he lifted up the front of his shirt just enough for Keyshawn to see all the Little Debbie cakes and chips he had lined across his waist. Then he handed a quarter to the clerk for a single bag of chips that he had in his hand. On his way out the door he turned to Keyshawn and said, "You better catch up man," laughing as he hit the street. He sat in the seat laughing to himself thinking back on that day. He couldn't help but wonder what Red was doing now. He hadn't seen him since he left Milwaukee. They had put their money together and bought a pound of weed and as they were on the way back to Red's house to bag it up, the police stopped them. The weed was found in the trunk of the car and since Red was the driver, it was his car, and Keyshawn had never been to the boys' home before, Red took the case. The only thing he said prior to the police walking toward the car was, "Don't trip, my nigga, if they find the weed I'll take the case, just make sure you send me some bread up to Wales." The relationship they had was deeper than just a friendship, they were like brothers. Never once had one of them crossed the other over a female, money, or anything shiesty that a lot of dudes did to their so-called *nigga*.

He made sure he sent fifty dollars every month to Red the entire year that he spent in jail. That was some real shit he had done by not letting them both take the fall and Keyshawn would never forget that. They also wrote each other from time to time, but neither was really the writing type so when they did write it wasn't much said really. Once Red got out, they talked several times a week for the first month, but that gradually slowed down to a couple times a month. And for the past six months (after he called Red's phone and the number wasn't working) they hadn't talked at all. However, he was sure that Red was still around because Keysha said that she saw him a few times.

He started to think about his sister; she was about to begin college at Marquette University this month, and he was very proud her. She had always been the smart one.

His thoughts were interrupted by a brief flow of turbulence; he took his headset off and looked around the plane and out the window for a second to make sure everything was alright. This was only Keyshawn's second time flying, so he wasn't really all that comfortable anyway.

With his headset back on, his grandmother crossed his mind. He was surely going to miss her. Especially her cooking, he rarely missed any of her meals.

Who he wouldn't miss however was his cousin Mal. He was part of the reason their grandmother was constantly catching Keyshawn in all his wrongdoings. Whatever Mal seen or heard about

Keyshawn he told her. It was hard not to get caught by Mal because he and his mother Trina lived with them.

The plane was now making a turn and he realized that they must have been getting ready to land. He turned his walkman off and started packing everything in his carryon bag. The captain was on the intercom again thanking everybody for flying United as the attendant walked down the aisle.

"You can power your cell phones back up now folks, thanks again for your cooperation," she said passing his seat.

He called his mother to let her know that he had arrived. As everyone began filing out of the plane, the Japanese couple was still talking and laughing in their native tongue; he couldn't help but wonder what the hell they were talking about that could be so funny for almost two and a half hours, this amused him.

He said goodbye to the crew, exited the plane, and headed for the terminal.

The airport wasn't all that busy on this night, so he was able to make it to baggage claim fairly quickly. Once he grabbed his luggage and made it to the U.A.'s pick up area outside Mitchell International Airport, his mom spotted him as she pulled up to the door. After putting his bags in the trunk, he got in to greet her. They hugged and she kissed him on the cheek before pulling off and heading toward Interstate 43.

"So, you must've made mama pretty mad, she called me at two o'clock in the morning telling me you would be on your way back home."

"I didn't know it was in my jacket, it fell out of my pocket when she picked it up off the couch," Keyshawn said.

"That's not the point; you shouldn't have had that stuff anyway, let alone in mama's house boy. I sent you down hoping you could get away from this mess up here and you take it right down there with you," Michelle said. "Well, I don't know what you gone do now that you back, you need to get a job or something since you don't want to finish school," she said shaking her head. "Your sister's about to be starting at Marquette, I'm so happy," she said smiling. "You and that girl are like night and day; hell, the only way I can tell ya'll are twins is by ya'll's looks."

They both started laughing, knowing it was true. He and Keysha had always been opposites in everything. What she liked, he hated and vice versa. As kids, they fought over everything constantly, but they still loved each other to death. All three of them did, they were all they had.

"Where's Keysha at anyway? Why she didn't come with you?" he said.

"She had to work, she get off at ten o'clock. She should be home not too long after we get there, baby. You know she got a little boyfriend now."

"You mean she *had* a boyfriend, cause I'm back now and she can't have no boyfriend, ma'."

"Keyshawn, don't come back here with that mess, that girl grown now," she said.

He had a displeased look on his face. "So," he said.

"I ain't playing with you, don't pull no stuff like you did with that boy; hell, I keep forgetting his name, but you know which one I'm talking about. The one you chased off that porch with that stick," she said. Keyshawn was laughing now. "I'm serious, you gotta get out of that, your sister's a young woman now. Plus, ain't nobody say nothing to you when you had that li'l ugly girl coming by the house eating dinner," she said laughing.

"Who Jada? She wasn't ugly, ma'," he said, looking at his mother with a smirk on his face.

"Yeah, whatever you say, she wasn't ugly." They both started laughing again.

"She was cool though, ma'."

"Yeah, I know she was a nice girl and looks don't mean everything," Michelle said warmly. They continued to talk on the way home, nothing serious, just chit chatting about what had been going on in Milwaukee while he was gone. They cruised along the highway until they came to the

9

McKinley Street exit. As they exited, the change in direction threw Keyshawn off guard.

"Ma', where you going?"

"Home."

"When you move?" he said, looking puzzled.

"I been moved Keyshawn, I told you this months ago. I see you still don't listen too well, just like Tim," she said shaking her head. "Speaking of which, have you talked to your father? she asked.

"Nope, not since the last time you asked me."

"Well…"

"Ma', I don't wanna talk about dude okay?"

Keyshawn had talked to his father once while he was in McComb. Tim lived in Detroit and hadn't really been a part of their lives, nor had he showed any interest to be. Keyshawn and Keysha longed for some kind of relationship with their dad, and Michelle knew this, so she tried to do everything in her power to fill that void they had in their lives. But she knew that was impossible as she, herself, had gone through the same thing growing up. Only her father wasn't absent by choice, he was killed in an accident when she was twelve years old. So, knowing how they felt, she tried her best to spoil them with love and whatever else they needed or wanted. Tim came in and out of the twins' life a few times; most recently was when they were thirteen years old. He came around for about a month or so, made a bunch of false promises and then like the deadbeat that he was, he disappeared again, only to call them every blue moon.

Sometimes Michelle cursed herself for having babies with such a bum; her sister would joke around occasionally saying, "Before you have kids by somebody there ought to be a law called, *The Deadbeat Daddy Test.*" Of course she was joking, but there was some seriousness there as well. Nonetheless, these were their kids and they were going to be alright, "With or without that nigga," as they would say to one another at times.

That was something that stuck with Keyshawn more so than any of his mother's teachings, "With or without" anybody else's help he was gone be alright; shit, they were all going to be fine and he would make sure of that. He was the man of the house and he was his own father, end of story.

As they continued driving to their destination, Keyshawn was wondering where they were going and where had she moved to until Michelle finally made a turn into Windsor Court, a nearby apartment complex, which was actually a low-income, government-funded project. Keyshawn was trying to figure out why they were here as they drove through the parking lot. There were a lot of kids out playing alongside young niggas dealing drugs and fiends looking for their next hit.

When Michelle parked the car Keyshawn looked over at her. "Ma', what's going on, you moved in here?" he said with a disgusted look on his face.

"Yeah baby, just come on inside. I want to talk to you about what else has been going on while you were away," she said, looking away pitifully.

Eager to talk, Keyshawn bolted to the trunk to grab his luggage. As he rushed by one of the young dealers who were posted outside the door as if he was holding down Fort Knox, he barely even noticed the fiend in the hallway by the stairs turning a date. As he walked down the hallway to the apartment, he couldn't help but smell the strong scent of piss that lingered throughout the air—an odor that all the residents had sadly become immune to smelling.

He entered the apartment and couldn't believe what he was seeing. It was like watching an old episode of Good Times, only this was no TV show. It was very much real and his mother and sister were living here.

He closed the door and walked around the small one bedroom that looked more like a studio compared to what they had been accustom to before he left. He put his bags down and sat on the couch next to his mother who was now smoking a cigarette. He had never seen Michelle smoking, and all sorts of horrific thoughts began racing through his head. He was thinking, *please don't tell me my mother's about to say she's on crack or my sister's somewhere dancing at some cheap ass strip club.* Trying to clear his thoughts, he looked over only to see a roach scaling the wall.

"Ma', what's going on, why are you living here?"

"I had no other choice Keyshawn. I lost my job after another company bought us out. They laid off three hundred workers and I happened to be one of them. That was about a year ago; what savings I did have in the bank, I started using to pay the mortgage at the old house. With all the bills we had over there, plus the mortgage, it didn't take long before the money I had in the bank was gone. So I started taking out loans to pay bills until that all dried up cause I had no money to pay them back, then I started falling behind on everything. The bank was calling threatening to foreclose on the house so I had to hurry up and sell it to at least get some of the equity back that I had in the place. And once I sold it, me and your sister had to move, so we moved here baby," she pulled hard on the Newport 100 then Keyshawn took a deep breath and exhaled.

Now he was thinking, *okay it's not as bad as I thought*, he started to ask her why she was smoking cigarettes, but thought that would have been a dumb ass question—it was obvious why.

"You okay, ma'?" he said in a worried tone.

"Yeah, I'm alright. You know life is full of valleys and peaks, baby; and I guess I just hit one of those valleys, that's all. But we'll be good, this is temporary," she said, trying to look re-assuring.

"Where is all your stuff, this ain't everything," he said.

"Oh our other things are in storage, which reminds me, I gotta pay those people this month before they start hounding me", she said sighing.

"How long you plan on staying here, ma'?"

"Well, right now I don't know," she said, blowing out the last of the cigarette smoke before putting it out. "When your sister got accepted to Marquette, you should have seen how happy she was Keyshawn," she said attempting to change the subject. "They only gave her a partial scholarship and she also got some grants and loans, but she still needed more money to cover other costs, so I paid that for her. I had to. I couldn't let my baby down, she's been waiting for this moment her whole life," she said as a tear rolled down her cheek.

Keyshawn reached over, hugged his mother, and wiped her face. "It's okay, ma', you did what you had to do," he said, praising his mother's unselfish act. When he released his mother, Keyshawn say a look on her face that he had never seen before, it was one of desperation and exhaustion.

"Why didn't you tell me y'all were going through all of this? I would've been came home, ma', you know that."

"I was gone tell you, but me and your grandmother talked about it, and I didn't want to worry you with something you couldn't do nothing about," she said, getting up and walking over to the kitchen. "You want something to drink? It's some Kool-Aid in here."

"Yeah, can you bring me a glass of ice water?" he asked.

"You and that damn water, boy, I've never seen a young person so serious about drinking water," she said laughing. "Me and Keysha were talking about yo' butt and that water the other day, that's good though, I don't know where you picked it up, but it's a good habit," she handed him the glass then headed toward the bedroom.

"When Keysha coming home, ma'?"

"She should be here in a minute, and Keyshawn please don't say anything to her about her school fees, I'll figure out a way to make sure it's all taken care of. We'll just have to take it one semester at a time."

"I won't. How is she getting around?" he said, finishing the water.

"Well, usually I'll drop her off at work and that boy will pick her up. If he can't, she'll call me and I'll get to her. You hungry?" she said, walking into the kitchen again. "Yeah, I'm starving. I ain't ate since this morning."

"I bet, mama told me you were down there eating everything in sight. And I see you've gained some weight since Christmas too."

Keyshawn didn't really hear her now; he was in the living room looking out the window wondering whose kids these were playing at almost ten o'clock at night by themselves.

Michelle came and stood next to him by the glass. "Those kids be out there all times of the night doing God knows what."

"I see," he said, staring at one of the little boys throwing rocks at passing cars. "What's in there to eat?"

"I made meatloaf and rice before I picked you up. I'll fix you a plate."

Keyshawn finished the food and was lying on the couch when he heard keys at the door. *It must be Keysha*, he thought, then leaned up straight enthusiastic about seeing his sister. When she walked through the door and saw him, she threw her purse on the floor screaming as she ran over to give her twin a hug. Keysha was always hyperactive; so this didn't surprise him.

"Hey, bro," she said.

"Girl, yo' loud self can wake up a whole block," Michelle said, walking out of her room.

"Hey, ma."

"What you do to your hair, girl?" Keyshawn said, trying to make out the dye color in her hair.

"Nothing, I just cut and colored it."

"What is that purple?" he said, flipping through her hair laughing.

"Yeah, don't hate nigga, it's my bossy look," she said, model posing now. The two of them looked nearly identical except for the fact that they were male and female. Keysha was a shade lighter than Keyshawn with a caramel brown complexion. They both had light brown eyes like Michelle, were nearly the same height, close to 5'9", with Keysha being the heavier of the two.

"Get outta here," Keyshawn said laughing. "Where's your little boyfriend? Why you didn't bring him in? What's his name?"

"His name is Brandon and he had to go that's why he didn't come up," she said smiling slyly.

"Yeah, right, you probably told him not to because you ain't want me to see him," he said grinning.

"Whatever dude, I know you bet not be on no bullshit cause he's a real cool person."

"Girl, I told you about that cursing," Michelle said from the bedroom.

"Dang, she hears everything," Keysha said whispering.

"I sure do, that's my job," Michelle said. They both busted out into laughter.

"Alright, ma', dang," Keysha said frowning up her nose jokingly. "So, what's up bro, you back home? I'm glad, I missed you dude."

"Nothing, I just was tripping a little bit when ma' brought me here earlier," he said, looking around.

"I know man, we need to move ASAP, and for real this place is a dump. People living here are crazy, you see all them dudes that be hanging out in the hallways looking thirsty as hell? Brandon said he think one of them was gone try to rob him the other night when he was leaving." "What, that's crazy," Keyshawn said.

"Yeah, I know, but hopefully we'll be out of here soon, mama said."

"We will, I'm gone make sure of that. So when you start school?" he said, changing the conversation.

"In two weeks, nigga. Yeah, Marquette, baby…haha," she was smiling and hitting Keyshawn on his arm.

"That's good sis, and maybe you can introduce me to some of your new buddies," he said smiling, knowing good and well that she wouldn't.

"Nope, cause you be on some bull and I always end up falling out with my friends over yo' ass dude," she said covering her mouth, hoping her mom didn't hear the curse word.

"Alright, forget you; your buddies always end up being some squares anyway. You seen Red lately?"

"Yeah, I seen him at the club a few weeks ago. That nigga thinks he slick as hell now, bro."

"Club? What club and what you doing in there?" he said surprised.

"How I get in you mean?"

"Yeah, how?" he was waiting for an answer.

"Come on dude, you can't be that slow; oh, I forgot you been in the sticks too long. Down there with grandma, I would have went crazy down there that long."

"Yeah, I bet, but you still ain't told me how you get in. Let me guess...fake ID, huh?"

"Ding, ding, ding. I see you ain't that slow after all, haha. And the club is called Matrix, it stays crackin', everybody goes there."

Keyshawn was tripping hearing some of these things coming from Keysha, once a super duper square who he couldn't get to steal their mother's car for a few hours at night while she was sleep. Now here she was talking about fake IDs, clubs, and calling him slow. He had to be gone too long, *what a difference two years could make,* he thought as he stared at her blankly for a brief moment.

"What?" she said.

"You."

"What about me?"

"Yo' ass done turned into a monster while I was gone," he said laughing.

"Mann...I be needing to do something to get away from this place, but I make sure I handles my

19

business before anything else, ya' dig," she said with a sly look.

"I feel you, sis."

They talked for a little while longer before Keysha announced that she was tired and going to bed. They both said goodnight as she went to lie down in the bed next to their mother.

It had been a long, interesting day. Keyshawn was doing an inventory of it all, with his mind set on one thing – getting his family back on track. He thought of his father and cursed him for lacking in manhood. Even if he wasn't with their mom, the least he could do was be there for him and Keysha. But he quickly blocked those thoughts out of his mind; he was a man now and refused to look at the situation any other way. His mother and sister desperately needed him to stand up and be accounted for, they didn't say this to him directly, but it didn't have to be said— look at the condition things were in. Yeah, he had to get something popping and there was no time for games. Here he was sleeping on a couch while his mother and sister shared a bed in that little ass room. Never in his entire life had they ever lived this way, and they weren't about to start now, not while he was breathing.

All kinds of thoughts ran through his head before he was finally able to fall asleep that night. Tomorrow and every day after that would be better and brighter. "Sink or swim" and he wasn't about to drown. It was time to find some "motivation" and be down for his crown.

Chapter 2

The following morning Keyshawn was up and at 'em. Sleeping on that couch wasn't a pleasant experience; his back and neck were both a little sore from being crunched up. But after a quick breakfast and a nice hot shower, he was dressed and ready to go.

Before he left in Michelle's car, he let Keysha know that he'd be back to get her in enough time for work. And on the way out the door he kissed his mother on the cheek, something he had a habit of doing since he was a shorty.

Walking through the hallway he caught another whiff of that pissy odor again, he curled up his nose, thinking that the smell wasn't something he could get accustom to.

Once outside, right away he noticed the neighbors were in full swing with what seemed to be their daily shenanigans. Paying it no mind, he jumped into the silver Dodge Intrepid and proceeded to exit the parking lot. Reaching the exit, the first thing he saw when he bent the corner, was a hot young number walking in the same direction he was headed. He almost forgot how beautiful Mil-town chicks were being away for two years, but this one here quickly refreshed his memory. She was short, chocolate, and thick with an ass so fat you could see it from the front! He was ready to spring into action just to see if he still had it. Back in McComb, pulling chicks was like driving to Keyshawn; he was simply way too fast for the locals down there. The biggest challenge he faced in the south was when he'd go to Jackson with his cousin Tap, and even that was a cake walk because the country girls loved his city swag.

He pulled over and rolled down the passenger window just as she was passing the front of the car.

"Hey sexy, how you doing, can I have a minute?" he said. One thing Keyshawn knew from experience was if that first sentence made a woman stop, he had her.

She stopped, glanced at him and said, "A minute for what?" with the sassiest look he'd ever seen. He was used to these kinds, the ones who try to play that, "what the hell you want" role. But he also knew to get out of the car at this point, it made chicks feel respected. A lot of young niggas didn't know that; but he learned from trial and error, always get out of the car once you had their attention. It was the least you could do, kind of like meeting them half way.

"A minute just to introduce myself," he said, walking over the curb. "I'm Keyshawn," he said, offering his hand.

She shook it and replied simply, "Quesha," with a smile.

"You live around here?" he said.

"I don't know, maybe."

"What is it a secret or something?"

"Nawh, but I don't know if I wanna tell you all that, especially with that loud ass orange shirt on," she said laughing.

"I been in Mississippi for the last couple of years and I just got back, so I guess I ain't up on Mil-town fashion just yet,"

"Oh, okay, I'm gone give you a pass this time then, but next time I see you, I hope you back in tune," she said smirking now.

"Who said I wanted to see you again?" he said, trying to look serious.

She laughed, "All okay, you had to get me back for that li'l shirt joke, huh."

"Right, aye, but I don't wanna hold you up any longer, you think I can call you?"

She agreed and they exchanged numbers.

"Alright, I'll hit you later. You don't need a ride or nothing do you?"

"Nawh, I'm good, thanks though, call me," she said as they parted ways.

Back in the car, he smiled to himself. Keyshawn always had his pick at what he wanted. And he knew the key to conversation that would get through to any female, it was simply being respectful.

He pulled off and headed for the barbershop, *and a clothing store*, he was thinking as he looked down at the bullshit he was wearing.

After stopping for a haircut, a nearby clothing store was next. He bought a few outfits and a couple pairs of shoes just to get his wardrobe back started. While he was putting everything in the trunk, Keysha called to tell him that she was with Brandon and he'd be taking her to work.

"Yeah, tell dude I still wanna meet him."

"Shut up nigga, bye," she said, laughing as she hung up the phone.

Keyshawn was enjoying the scenery as he rode through the city, some things had changed; he noticed there had been lots of new homes and buildings going up all over the place. The mayor and city council had finally taken the initiative to invest some money in the ghetto in an attempt to bring up low-income neighborhoods and business districts that once thrived but lost their appeal over the years. It was a start, but plenty of work still needed to be done.

Of course, none of this was an issue to Keyshawn; no matter how dingy or torn up certain parts of the city looked, it was still home to him and it was beautiful.

He got to the intersection of Keefe, Atkinson, and MLK Drive; there he made the left turn to hit Atkinson Avenue. Nothing looked any different except for a new service station that was placed on

8th street by the Arabs in an effort to steal clientele from the black owned one directly across the street. Sadly, the locals were too simple to see the politics of it all. Johnson's was a much smaller operation compared to the Arabs, and the Arabs generally carried a larger selection of goods. But whatever happened to unity and community, the Johnson's had been operating there for twenty years. Still no one seemed to care about any of this.

Passing the neighborhood park, he noticed that the park house had been removed and the entire playground looked neglected and deserted. Something that the local alderman should have been very committed to, but was probably too busy shaking down district business owners and taking bribes.

Keyshawn was looking at all this through fresh eyes, but even he couldn't see the relevant issue of what really lied beneath the surface of the happenings in the hood. But how could he, he was much too young to understand or even take interest in any of these issues.

As he approached the corner of Atkinson and 13th, he noticed some familiar faces off to his right a short distance down the block. Many of them were a part of the Smith family. They had numerous affiliates, a lot of whom had been amongst them for decades now. So long that no one outside of their inner circle knew who was who, so they labeled them all Smiths. To them, they were all family; it was them against the city and they carried it that way. Ranging from crap-shooters to pimps, gangsters, robbers and thieves, to D-boys, diplomats, and all-around players…just about every real element of the streets was in these niggas' bag. Keyshawn had come up a few years under some of the older nephews, so they were the ones he mostly had a connection with.

"Hey, what's up, baby?" T.A. said as Keyshawn was crossing the street in the direction of the crowd. "I see they let you off punishment, huh?" T.A. said laughing.

"Yeah, whatever nigga, what's up, T?" Keyshawn said as they had a quick embrace.

"Mane, nothing much, 'bout to smash on this li'l hoe of mine and pick up these earnings in a minute." T.A. always had something slick to say when you saw him no matter when, where, or what time of the day you caught him, he was in a cheery mood. He, Keyshawn and Red got tight back when they both started selling weed. They copped from T.A. and he always looked out for 'em because he liked to see young niggas motivated to get some cash.

"When you get back in town?" T.A. said, playing with the diamond-encrusted Rolex on his wrist.

"Yesterday, I was so glad to get the hell out of that little ass town, my nigga," Keyshawn said, shaking Bone's hand as he was walking up.

"What's to it, mack buddy?" Bone said, shaking a pair of dice in his left hand. This nigga Bone was what you would call a swindler. He was known for having at least five racks on him at any given time, all from a good day of hustling. Knowing him, he was no doubt about to be on his way to trim some unlucky suckers shortly. He crap-hustled during the day, partied at night, and pimped 24/7 cause he kept his hoes on automatic.

"Shit, man, I see you still breaking these niggas, huh?" Keyshawn said, shaking his head laughing.

"Don't forget these bitches now, I break them too, you know," Bone said, laughing at his own humor.

"Dig that," Keyshawn said, looking over at Fat Boy. "I see you don't know a nigga no more, huh Fat Dog," he said, throwing his hands in the air.

"I was waiting for them two dudes to get done talking shit, what's up, li'l homie?" Fat Boy was giving Keyshawn some dap. He was a serious nigga who rarely joked around or played games. He specialized in twistin' niggas out of town for big licks. He kept a crew of young niggas who idolized him and his teachings, and they loved him to death cause he had them eatin' well. The only vice Fat Boy had was an addiction to high-end designer clothes. But it was nothing and he could stand to buy what he wanted. From Gucci to Fendi, Feragamo and Loui V., this nigga had to be undisputedly the best dressed robber in the city.

The crazy thing was, Keyshawn had known him for at least ten years now and never understood where he got his name because he wasn't fat. He actually only weighed about a hundred twenty pounds soaking wet.

Keyshawn made his way around to greeting everybody before he ventured back over to T.A. to discuss some business. T.A. was in his cocaine-white Jag with matching white interior. A sight that looked rather funny to Keyshawn because T.A. was black as a muthafucka.

He got in, the AC was blowing heavily, it was near the end of summer, but Wisconsin had some funny weather and today was beginning to be hot already.

"You got something to do, dawg?" T.A. said, throwing the Jag in gear.

"Nawh, why what's up?" Keyshawn was fiddling with the CD player now.

"Alright, I'm bout to ride down on this hoe and scrap up these funds," T.A. said, pulling off from the curb. "How yo' mama doing, man? I see they moved from down the block."

"All yeah, she doing okay," he said, going through the CD case.

"I seen Keysha li'l ass out at the club on East Capitol a couple of times," T.A. said.

"I told her not to be hanging out in them clubs, that shits for these sluts."

"Yeah, but she be straight, you know if I'm ever around I got her, y'all like family, Key."

"I know, dawg; aye, who is this nigga?" Keyshawn said, pulling out a CD from the case.

"That's this nigga out the Mil name Baby Drew," he said, glancing at the CD.

Keyshawn popped the CD in the player and turned the volume up just enough so they could still hear one another and chop it up.

"So, now that your back, what you plan on doing, young player?" T.A. said, firing up a blunt of hydro while they sat at a street light.

"I'm bout to get at this money; shit, what else is it to do, mane."

"Go to school nigga, that's what…so you can be a doctor or a lawyer one day," T.A. said, looking at him before he hit the blunt. They both started laughing.

"It's too late for that shit, T."

"Tell me about it. I'm out here in this shit, ain't no turning back. At twenty-three I'm just getting started, baby," he said as he was starting to feel the effects of the dro now. He attempted to pass the blunt to Keyshawn, but caught himself. "My fault, fam…I forgot you don't mess with this shit," he said, adjusting himself in the seat slightly.

"I'm gone tell you one thing though Key, it's time to elevate the game for real baby," T.A. said, blowing out some smoke.

Keyshawn knew he was high now, he'd been around T.A. long enough to know when he was feeling himself, and right now was one of those moments. *All man, I can only imagine what he's about to say to this chick once we get over here*, he was thinking to himself. "I hear you, dawg," he said, waiting to be amused some more.

"Aye, straight up, nigga...I'm bout to put these hoes on this new game, this internet shit, my Pops building me a website right now. It's a new millennium Key, and I'm bout to have some new game, new jewels, and a fresh Jag out these hoes ass. Yeah, these rapping niggas ain't got shit on T.A., my nigga. I can sell them cats some lines and I bet that shit go platinum."

Keyshawn was laughing hard as hell now. *Oh yeah, who ever this broad is she was about to be in for a real treat cause this nigga was in rare form now.*

"You still be having that good burner, fam?" he said, ready to get down to business.

"You know I do playa, what you need to hold something? I got a few pounds I can throw you 'til you get yo' money back up."

"Nawh, I'm good. I got a couple dollars, I was thinking about buying a few of 'em from you." Keyshawn didn't like for niggas to hand him shit, he always prided himself on hustling and making his own way. Besides, he wasn't broke; he had a nice li'l operation going in McComb with the weed.

"Okay, you musta' been down there getting it in with the country folks?"

"A li'l bit, you know a nigga wasn't gone stop eating homie."

"You know what though, Key…you need to get it up and start fucking with these hoes. Fuck that bag; make these funky bitches get their hands dirty. Shit man, these li'l young tramps dying for a player to bring 'em out the dirt."

Keyshawn was taking it all in, he never entertained the thought of pimpin' although he knew he had a way with words and chicks always did love his swag.

"You know that nigga Red finally came home and put his P down. He got a salt and pepper team. He ain't been coming to the store lately, so them hoes must be doing something slick for the nigga man," T.A. said, finally putting the blunt out in the ashtray.

"Man, where my nigga at? I ain't talked to him in months."

"I got his number, hold up, let me run in here real quick," T.A. said, exiting the vehicle.

Keyshawn turned up the radio. The rapper was saying something about walking on water and being Mr. Gold Fingers and he was grooving, but at the same time, being very much aware of his surroundings. They had come to one of the most impoverished parts of the city near 23rd and Locust, and you could never be too careful in Milwaukee. He was pretty sure T.A. had a banger on him because that was a part of his MO, but hell, what good was it gone do him he was in the house. He felt like a fly in a milk bowl sitting in this white ass Jag rimmed up with no heat. He saw some kids playing across the street, but his attention was more focused on a group of young characters who were looking like they were just itching to make a name for themselves.

A few more minutes had passed and T.A. was finally coming out. He was carrying a small Gucci bag in his hand while talking on the phone with the other. Once he got in and drove off, Keyshawn saw the magazine of a black glock poking out of his pocket. "Man, every time I come over here those li'l niggas be all in my glamour like they want some action at a player dawg," he said, putting the bag on the floor. "I'm bout to move my people from over here though. I got two of my bitches staying there. They been humping hard for me, man…so I think I'm gone move ''em down by the lake somewhere in the next couple of months," he said studying the road. "I'm 'bout to stop by the house to drop off this change and get something to eat."

"Cool, aye…call that nigga Red," Keyshawn said, leaning back in the passenger seat. T.A. pulled Red up in his phone and hit the send button before he handed the cell phone to Key. There was no answer.

"That nigga ain't pick up," Keyshawn said, passing the phone back to T.A.

"That figures, he never does, he'll be calling back in a minute," he said, switching lanes.

Chapter 3

They arrived to T.A's place a few short minutes after exiting the freeway. When they pulled up to the building, he punched in a security code into a keypad near the wall of the building before they were able to enter into the underground area.

He parked next to a convertible white Cadillac XLR. "I just copped her a month ago," he said, patting on the hood. "This is what I play in at night around this muthafucka."

Keyshawn wasn't surprised. T.A. had been known for driving the sickest shit in town since he was a young teen.

They got on an elevator that dropped them off on the tenth floor. T.A. was telling Keyshawn about a white chick that stayed two doors down from him whom he had been macking on. When she bought him the Rolex he was wearing, she had insisted on having it sprayed before he put it on his wrist. Awh, she was indeed his kind of chick, and when she wanted to play, she knew she had to pay.

The door to the condo was set up with a keyless entry pad. When they went in, Keyshawn took a seat on the couch, grabbed the remote and began surfing the cable channels while T.A. headed for his bedroom upstairs. The place was fit completely for a young king. With a price tag of $2,200 a month, the luxurious building (dubbed Kilbourn Towers) was located near the downtown area. Furnished with thick, cream carpeting throughout the place, equipped with state-of-the-art appliances, mahogany wood trimmings, a sunken living room, plush Italian furniture, and a pool table off to the side with a wet bar. T.A.'s bedroom was upstairs with a balcony overlooking the living room; he had a full bathroom connected to his room along with a spacious walk-in closet. Spending top dollar putting this place together, he could have nothing but the best. It was a long way from the hood. There he kept another spot that he utilized for business purposes. His pops, Moe, was an old school player who advised him to never mix the streets with his home if he wanted to sleep comfortable at night. So the only people who knew where he lived were in his immediate circle. Red and Keyshawn were apart of that, they were like his li'l brothers and he would trust them both with his life if need be.

Once he secured the money in the safe under his bed, he was on his way back down stairs when his phone rang. It was Red. "What's up baby?" T.A. said, walking to the balcony. "Aye, Key…this Red right here."

"What's happenin', cool? That nigga Key back in town, huh?" Red said with excitement.

"Yeah," T.A. said, heading back down stairs. "Let me holla' at my nigga."

"Aight," he took the phone to Keyshawn and went into the kitchen.

"Say nigga, what's to it?" Keyshawn said, watching some thick video chick doing an interview on *106 & Park*. He didn't know which one was the baddest, her or the host Free.

"Just standing on these hoes necks, getting my cock sucking cash out they ass."

"Yeah, I been hearing good things about you, where you at my nig?"

"I'm leaving out of Racine on my way back to Milwaukee. I was getting some gas when y'all called.

"Tell that nigga to shot thru here," T.A. said, making a sandwich.

"We down here at T's crib, I'm bout to smash this dude in some chess, stop down when you get off the highway."

"Aight, I'll be there in about a half hour," Red said before hanging up.

"You wanna try yo' luck at some chess? Come on now, you know you can't fuck in mine, young nigga," T.A. said.

Keyshawn had never beaten him yet, but he was always up for the challenge. The chess board was already set up on a marble table behind the couch. Keyshawn was at the table now ready to test his skills. He turned the TV up. "You think that nigga,

A.J., fucking that bitch Free dawg?" Keyshawn said, studying the screen.

"Hell nawh, that square ass nigga look gay. I'd be hitting that bitch, right along with her pockets." T.A. said, laughing but serious as ever. "Them TV chicks ain't no different than any other dame, they all want a nigga with some flava homie," T.A. said, sitting at the table now.

"Right, you know who's a bad bitch though, that Alicia Keys chick," Keyshawn said, reaching for some chips off of T.A.'s plate.

"Haha, yeah, I know you wouldn't mind having a go at that. See once you get past the looks, you gone be a cold nigga. You and everybody else want a shot at that li'l bitch, so her nose stuck up as high as this building we sitting in right now. I'll take the bitch, but she wouldn't be my first round pick. Give me a bitch like Oprah."

"Oprah! Her old ass man," Keyshawn said laughing.

"See, that's the beauty of it, she got plenty money and I bet she gone make sure a young player like me stay in order."

Keyshawn was still laughing, he understood the science behind T.A.'s words, but the thought of Oprah and this nigga together was the funny part.

"Yeah, keep laughing youngin, I bet yo' ass wouldn't be snickering if I pulled up in a new Bentley joint with that fat bitch and them two black ass dogs she got," T.A. said laughing to himself.

"Yeah, I'd like to see you pull that one off nigga," Keyshawn said, reaching for half of a sandwich from T.A.'s plate.

"Never underestimate the power of this izum lil nigga. And take yo' ass in the kitchen, its food in there, while you steady sneaking shit off my plate."

"It's yo' move," Keyshawn said chewing.

They were on the second game of chess when Red called T.A.'s phone to get buzzed into the building. The first one had been a battle; T.A. nearly lost his long standing undefeated record against Key. And this one was no different. Red was at the door hitting the bell.

"Hold up so I can let this nigga in," T.A. said, racing to the door. This was a good game so he wanted to hurry and get back to it.

"Kick your shoes off pimp," T.A. said, turning around and heading back to the table.

"Say, mane, these Gucci sandals playa," Red was full of himself. "And they smell like pussy too," he said as he was kicking them off.

"I don't care what they smell like, last time you came in here tracking shit on the floor," T.A. said moving his bishop.

"Y'all niggas playing, that's why this dude moving so fast. My nigga!!" Red said as Keyshawn was getting up to greet him.

"What's going on?" Keyshawn said, happy to see his homie. They shared an unbreakable bond and nothing had changed. Even after two years of not seeing one another, they both still felt that same love from the other.

"I'm glad you back, dawg. I see you still be moving them pieces, huh."

"Yeah, a lil bit," Keyshawn said, concentrating.

"He all up in yo' house T," Red said, referring to Keyshawn's position on the board.

"Man, this nigga done stepped his game up for real," T.A. said now moving a rook over to Keyshawn's side of the board. "Check. But he still ain't all the way ready. I keep telling y'all niggas I took lessons from Bobby Fisher in Germany," T.A. was obviously joking.

"Yeah right, you ain't been to no damn Germany. I'm glad somebody else around to play this nigga now." Red said, going in the kitchen.

"Tired of getting yo' ass whooped, huh?" T.A said laughing.

"Nawh, hold up, you know I'll get with you nigga," Red said, walking back into the living room with a glass of orange juice.

"Check," Keyshawn said, feeling rejuvenated.

"Look like you got enough trouble on yo' hands already," Red said, sitting on the couch tuning into the TV.

T.A. was trying to figure a way out of check that wouldn't put him in any more danger, but he didn't have many options, he was stuck.

"Yeah nigga, you know what it is, it's a rap," Keyshawn said, seeing victory close by.

"Hold up," T.A. was looking for the right move. He couldn't find any, he only had two and neither looked promising. Knowing what was coming next; he moved his king out of check and waited for the call.

"Checkmate!" Keyshawn said, smiling now.

"What?" Red said, rushing over to the table. "Hell nawh, this nigga really is getting good at this shit," he said studying the board.

To the three of them, this day was history. And it was monumental for Keyshawn as he was still grinning.

"Good game, nigga. This cat done went down there and enrolled in chess school or something," T.A. said, shaking Keyshawn's hand. "Who you been playing dawg?" T.A. was still amazed by his new skills.

"My cousin Tap, he play this shit for money, it's his hustle." And he did, Tap broke the entire game down to Keyshawn piece by piece, even gave him books and magazines on how to improve his game.

"I'm gone have to meet that nigga," T.A. said, putting the pieces back in their starting positions. "You wanna play another one?" T.A. said eager to break the tie.

"Let's take a break for a minute man, my brain needs a rest," Keyshawn said rubbing his temples. He loved chess, but T.A. was a fiend, he could play it all day if he had nothing else to do. But this was his mental exercise; "Chess is a thinking man's game," his father often told him that when T.A. would play with him as a kid.

"Alright, we one and one, I got the next one though," was T.A.'s words as they both rose up from the table.

Red was at the couch counting money on the table when Keyshawn came and sat down.

"I see things been looking up for you, dawg; that's good," he said, kicking his feet on the ottoman.

"Yeah man, after I got out of Wales I been trying to be more careful. That was some bullshit in there Key; I'm never trying to see no jail shit again, fam. That's why I slowed pushing that bag. A nigga last longer pushing pussy instead."

"I feel you. So what you be doing, just sending 'em to work or what?" Keyshawn said inquisitively.

"Sometimes, but I'm hands on, taking them hoes outta here myself you know. For some reason, I love that highway, and my bitches love when I'm with 'em, seems like they work extra hard. T.A. sat back just listening, sure Red was right; they worked harder when a nigga was on out there in the trenches with 'em. But what worker wouldn't kick it up a notch in the presence of the boss?! A bitch was no different in his eyes, she aimed to please one person, her pimp, and she knew that the only real way to please a pimp was by producing more and more money. You didn't have to

Mexican pimp or escort her to get your money; all you had to do was get her to understand you weren't accepting anything less than the best. And the best meant the best hoes on the globe, because the best hoes got the best results making you the best pimp in the game. However, he didn't learn this overnight, it took him some years to get his pimping to the level where it was; and Red was a qualified young player who possessed the same potentials, if not more. Not to mention the fact that he was doing excellent in comparison to most pimps his age.

T.A. figured he'd let his li'l homies talk, knowing that they had much catching up to do after two years. He went out on the terrace to suck in some fresh air and check out the view. In six months of living here, he could count on one hand how many times he'd been out there. But that's how the street life was, you attain a lot of shit and most of the time you can't even enjoy any of it because you're too busy chasing after additional shit.

"Where you working your folks at?"

"An assortment of places, I'm mainly in Chicago though, it's a few tracks over there that a bitch can really get paid on. But if I ain't over there, I might hit up Detroit and do Michigan Avenue, a bitch getting at least two hundred a date over there; them tricks pay good. When I go there, I may stay for a month or two to paper up real nice on 'em. After that, I'll come back and take a break; let my work sit down for a couple of days but no more than that. Then I'll ship 'em somewhere, a pimp can't allot a whore too much relaxation cause they'll start getting lazy. I found that out the hard way when I lost a bitch to another pimp cause she was so used to working and I began to slack up on the tramp, my nigga. But you know a player learn from his mistakes though."

Keyshawn wasn't amazed at how fast Red had adopted to life as a pimp. Back when they were kids, Red was the first one to learn how to shoot dice and play cards with a stacked deck. He also presented the idea to Keyshawn that since he was so good at ping pong, why not get paid for his talent. They had a system in place where Red would bring the action, Keyshawn would let the vic win a game or two, and then Red would make a wager with Keyshawn betting him that he would lose. This always caused the vic to want in on the action. And once he started betting, if he stayed long enough, he'd eventually lose all of his money. This was a huge hustle for two eleven-year-old kids.

"I hear you, I'm 'bout to jump down with these greens, that's why I'm over here fucking with this nigga T. I'm tryna get it like you niggas. I leave and come back, you got diamonds in shit all in your mouth, pimpin' hoes. This nigga T. wearing frost bit Rollies living on the lake with galleries in shit everywhere," he said, pointing to the one overlooking the living area. "What the hell's going on here?" Keyshawn said laughing.

"I know, I told pimp buddy he living slick as hell down these ways. Did he tell you about snow white down the hall?" Red said grinning.

"Man, you know he had to throw that one at me right away," Keyshawn said still laughing. "That niggas a muthafucka ain't he?"

"Yep. Aye, but dawg, do you need anything man?"

"Nawh, I'm good my nigga,"

"You sure...cause yo' ass look like you could use a new shirt," Red said jokingly.

"Whatever man, I went and did a lil shopping this morning. This lil broad tried to roast me about this shirt earlier today too," he said, adjusting his collar.

"I bet she did."

"Awh, I see you tryna get off, I'll be getting it together though nigga," Keyshawn said smiling.

"I know fam, I'm just messing with you. I need to get going. I still got a few things to do," Red said as they were getting up from the couch. They went to the balcony; T.A. was sitting on the patio set that he'd purchased when he moved in.

"I'm 'bout to hit it, playboy," Red said shaking T.A.'s hand.

"Aight, dawg. What you doing later on? Maybe we can take this nigga somewhere since he just got back in town."

"Okay, that's cool, I'ma get up with y'all later on then."

"I need to be getting up too; you ready to go handle that business, Key?" T.A. said reluctantly. He was really enjoying the peace and serenity of the atmosphere out on the patio. The lake looked good from this view; before they came out, he was watching some people lying out on a yacht...some shit that he'd yet to experience, but he told himself that he soon would.

"Yeah, I need to check and see what up with moms anyway. I been in her car all morning," Keyshawn said.

When they made it back to Atkinson, T.A. had one of his chicks meet him there; she pulled up in a tan Nissan Altima. He got in the car and quickly emerged with a black duffle bag as she pulled off.

"Just give me $500 a piece, dawg; it should be like ten of 'em in here," he said, placing the bag on the passenger seat floor.

"I'ma holla at you later, baby...and drive smooth with this shit in here man."

"Aight, my nigga, later," Keyshawn said, putting the car in gear.

On the way to his mother's place, he was nervous as hell. All he kept thinking about was the last time him and Red busted that move and got pulled over with this shit. But he played it cool, he had a license to drive this time, so he just put his seat belt on and did his best to forget about the ten pounds of weed he had in the car.

Once he finally pulled into the parking lot of the project buildings, he could breathe a little better. He grabbed the duffle bag and the shopping bags that he had in the trunk. He didn't want to look odd carrying just a duffle bag in the building, especially with all the people that were hanging outside of these buildings. No one knew him, so naturally he was already sticking out like a sore thumb. A few people gave him the eye, but he casually breezed through with no static. Once in the apartment, he just sat everything in the corner of the living room. Keysha was watching TV and talking on the phone.

"What you doing here, I thought you got off at ten, sis?" he said sitting down.

"I only had a half day today."

"Where mama at?" he said, being conscious of the weed he bought into the house.

"She went somewhere with Aunt Hazel. Why you whispering?"

"Oh, okay. Check it out, I got some greens in this bag, where should I put it?" he said, opening the bag to look at the product and check its quality.

"Damn, yo ass just back up here last night, you ain't waste no time I see," she said shaking her head.

"I ain't tryna' to hear that girl," he said, smelling one of the packages. They were all compressed pounds of highgrade lime green regular. Keyshawn was doing the math now; he knew that with this type of quality he could easily get $1,200 a piece giving him a $7,000 profit. He also knew that T.A. couldn't have been making much of nothing at the price that he quoted to him. Which he wasn't, T.A. was getting a hundred pounds from his Mexican plug in Chicago at $400 a pound. So he was only making a $1,000 but Keyshawn was his lil brother and he wanted to see him eating.

"Just put it in that closet over there on the top shelf, mama never goes in there, all my stuff is in that one and she uses the one in the room," Keysha said wondering where he got all this weed, but she figured it had to be T.A. or one of the other Smiths cause they were the only people her brother fucked with like that.

"You know Brandon be selling that stuff sometimes; he probably can move some of it for you," she said.

"Yeah, do he be handling a lot of it or just small shit?"

"He don't be having as much as what's in that bag, but I've seen him with a few of them."

Now this was music to his ears. He figured this nigga was probably buying a couple of pounds. And since he was getting this shit so cheap from T.A., he could give the nigga some sweet numbers to make sure he'd fuck with him. But first he had to find out more about this dude.

"How long have you been messing with this cat, sis? You think I can trust him like that?" he said looking at Keysha closely.

"Bro, Brandon is a square; he go to college at UWM, work a job, and only sells to people he goes to school or grew up with in Glendale. Plus, he loves me; he would never do anything to hurt you," she said smiling because she knew how Brandon felt about her.

He liked the fact that Keysha knew so much about this guy. And he also knew that she was no dummy. Over the years, they had both laced one another about the opposite sex and she always knew more than Keyshawn did.

"Okay, when can I talk to him?"

"He'll be over here once he gets off work. He's cool, I'm telling you, you ain't got nothing to worry about." Keysha loved Brandon, and she knew how Keyshawn could be overprotective sometimes, so she just wanted them to get off to a good start. "You eat yet?" she said.

"Nawh, what you hungry or something?"

"Yeah man, you gone take me to get something to eat?"

"You can take yourself, you got a license."

"Come on, bro, I don't feel like driving," she said. Keysha hadn't hung out with her brother in a long time and she just wanted to kick it with him.

Keyshawn sensed this. "Come on," he said, patting her on the leg.

Chapter 4

The club was packed nearly to capacity as a busty white waitress worked her way through the crowd serving drinks and taking tips. You could barely see over the mob that grew around the stage as this week's feature dancer gave them the best show of the night so far. Niggas were throwing every bill they could find in their pockets, as the amazon was hanging upside down on the pole, swallowing a rubber black twelve-inch dildo. She slid all the way down, got on all fours and proceeded to fuck herself with the exotic instrument. One of the spectators tried to climb on stage, but was subdued by security before he could make it. By now, she was laying on her back with both her legs wrapped around her neck like a pretzel as she screwed herself and came at the same time. Before finishing with her show, she took the shaft out of her pussy to suck and lick it up one last time before getting on her knees to scoop up all the money that her talent had earned her. Then she blew a kiss at the crowd before going to the dressing room to freshen up and change for her next set.

Meanwhile, at the rear of the joint in a private section, T.A. and Red were holding a respectable player's review on the difference between *ass shakers* and *stomp down concrete whores*, while sipping on Remy XO and Dom P. Keyshawn was drinking on an *easy living*, he'd tried drinking, but it wasn't his bag, so he stayed drug and alcohol free.

"See, mane…the only way I could fuck with an entertainer bitch—as they so-call call themselves—is if she's working in a spot where she's got the green light to sell some pussy," T.A. said, noticing one of the performers checking him out from across the room.

"If a bitch can't get down how she needs to, it ain't worth the hoe working there for eight hours. Then she gotta line up dates for the end of the night, that's if it's some action in the muthafucka! Hell nawh, pimp, mine ain't going," Red said with a look of disgust.

"Yeah, like the goofy ass tramp who just came off stage sticking objects all up in her funky ass doing flips in shit. Them cheap ass niggas ain't give her enough bread for all that! I wish I would catch one of my hoes on that kick, it better not be a small bill nowhere near the pile. I'd break that bitch's face for disrespecting my pimpin' in that manner," T.A. said scoping the same chick jockin him again. Then suddenly, she mustered up enough courage to act on her interest as she came walking up and placed her arm on his shoulder.

"Damn, baby, you over here looking like I did something wrong. A bitch know who you are, I was deciding if I wanted to test the waters or not," she said.

MOTIVATION: MASTERING THE GAME

"Sure you can hoe, after you bless a pimp with his propers."

"And how much is that, with yo' fine black ass?" she said, stroking his shoulder.

"If it's enough to count, it ain't enough for me. But I'll tell you what, you come with what you think you're worth and I'll see if it's sufficient."

"Well, you got a number or something so I can call you when I get off work?" she said with a seductive smile. He handed her a business card and she tucked it in her money bag.

"I'll be calling you," she said walking away. T.A. gave no response; he simply turned around and continued his conversation. After all, it was a privilege for a bitch to even get that much dialogue from him without cash on delivery.

"That bitch was all on a pimp's wood, but her presentation was no good," T.A. said laughing. "How that hoe gone dive in the paint like that on a pimp with no currency in tow?" he asked Red.

"You shoulda' told that bitch to go home and find her hoe manual and look up *the proper approach when choosing a pimp,*" Red said, raising his glass.

"Right, I think it's the first page in Chapter 1, fool ass bitch," T.A. said as they slapped their glasses together.

Keyshawn was enjoying the show. He may not have had any input, but he sure was getting a kick out of these two niggas. In fact, he was enjoying the entire experience. This was his first time in a strip club. He and Red weren't even old enough to be in the place. But Red had been frequenting these types of establishments since he'd been released from Wales. And age made no difference as he

quickly found that any doorman could be bought.

Keyshawn's phone began vibrating; the number on his screen was an unfamiliar one to him so he got up and went into the restroom to answer it.

"Hello," he said, wondering who the caller was.

"I see you was jackin' about calling, huh?" she said, it was Quesha, the chick he'd met earlier. He recognized the voice.

"Nawh, it ain't like that. I just been busy all day. I was gonna call you though."

"Damn, I feel like I'm sweating you or something. You busy right now?" she said feeling rejected.

"A little bit, I'll call you back in a minute alright?" he said as other people were entering the restroom.

"Okay, bye."

"Aight, later."

When he walked out of the door, a girl grabbed his arm. "Hey honey, you want to buy a lap dance?" she said, rubbing her tits on his arm.

"Nawh, I'm good baby."

Pimp or no pimp he was no sucka.

The feature dancer was on her way to them as she was working the crowd for more tips. She walked between Red and T.A. smelling money, because both of them were iced out from eye and ear wear to wrist wear.

"How y'all doing tonight, fellas? Did you guys see my show?"

Her stage name was Toya Rider; she stood about 5'10" without heels, caramel complexion with hair down to her ass. Her waist was 26" and she had enough ass to put Buffie the Body to shame.

MOTIVATION: MASTERING THE GAME

"Did you happen to see either one of us over there?" Red said, being the first to respond.

"No, baby, it was so many people, I couldn't possibly make everybody out."

Yeah this bitch was definitely full of herself, Red was thinking. This hoe actually had the audacity to entertain the thought that he might have been around a stage gazing at her like he was one of these dollar throwing chumps. All yeah, it was time to slice this bitch up.

"Say, baby…dig this, obviously you ain't from around here, cause if you were you would know that you're in the mist of some boss pimps and you in direct violation. This time, I'm gonna give you a pass; but you pull a stunt like this again and I'ma break you and send yo' ass to work. And I can guarantee you it won't be no cozy place like this here, yo' ass gonna be humping for real."

She strolled away with a pitiful look on her face. But Red didn't give a shit, he was a pimp and she was a hoe. That's the nature of the game, when a bitch got out of pocket she had to be checked immediately. This was one of his keys to being a strong pimp. Either a bitch was gone accept it or reject it; but regardless her choice, she would damn well respect it. Bottom line, there was no room for soft pimps; whores honored the ones that went hard on a bitch and ruled with iron fists.

T.A. sat back smiling when she walked off, he was proud of the seeds he'd planted in this young nigga, they were blossoming well. He knew Red was on his way to being a heartless pimp with ice water running through his veins.

Keyshawn soaked up every word. Processing the

49

points and principles of everything Red and T.A. kicked about the pimping.

They'd screened almost every chick in the place. And both came to a mutual consensus; with the exception of a few, there really wasn't any action here tonight, they spent another hour talking shit. By this time, they'd all grown tired of the scene and were ready to go.

Chapter 5

Early the next morning, the first thing Keyshawn did was picked up a rental car. He had plenty to get started on and didn't need to be restricted in his movement.

Brandon had assured him when they met that he could move a large portion of the weed for him with no problem. So he was the first person he called once he got in traffic. He asked him to meet him at Perkins for breakfast while they discussed a few things.

Keyshawn arrived first, sitting in a booth for two. He informed the waitress that someone else would be arriving shortly. She set the table up for two before hurrying off to greet another customer. Perkins was a black-owned and ran soul food restaurant. Keyshawn had been eating here since he was a kid. It was in the neighborhood and they had good food.

When Brandon arrived, the waitress was bringing water to the table. Brandon was dressed like most college students did. He wore jogging pants with a UWM T-shirt and Adidas sandals. With an athletic build, he worked out religiously and ran track for the school as well.

"She take your order yet?"

"Nawh, I just walked in right before you."

"Okay," he said as he studied the menu.

"I talked to a few of my people last night. A buddy of mine wants to know if he can get four of 'em for $4,500? I'ma grab three for myself. And some other people wanna grab a single or two. But that's gone be later today."

Liking this dude already, Keyshawn said, "We can do that, as a matter of fact I'll give you ten for an even ten Gs, that's if you get 'em all today."

He really wanted to get as close to $12,000 as possible. But more than anything, he wanted to get rid of the package as soon as possible and figured if he gave them to Brandon at this number, he would come back and fuck with him. Plus, T.A. had informed him last night on their little outing that it was getting dry on the greens in Milwaukee. Which meant numbers would rise throughout the city and if Brandon had this type of clientele he needed him on his team.

"Cool," Brandon said.

* * * * *

When Keyshawn made his way to the twenty-story tower, T.A. was working out. He threw the bundle of cash on the floor where T.A. was doing sit-ups.

"Man, I know you ain't dumped all that shit this quick?" T.A. said surprised.

"I'm grinding, my nigga," Keyshawn said smiling.

"It ain't even two o'clock, and I know you didn't move none yesterday."

"I'm on it, baby."

"I see. So I guess you need some more, huh?"

"Fa sho, dawg."

"Alright, but them numbers gone have to go up a couple dollars. Otherwise, I won't be making nothing, you dig?"

"I know, dawg, and I appreciate you doing that for me big homie."

After a little negotiating, they agreed on $750 a piece and Keyshawn was happy with that.

"You know I'm only doing this cause you my man, I'd have to have top dollar if you were anybody else cause that shit is some bag." T.A. went upstairs. He came back wiping off the sweat with a bath towel. "You know that dame broke bread wit' a player last night right."

"Which one you talking about?"

"The Puerto Rican one who I gave my card to at the club," T.A. said.

"Dig that?"

"Yeah, dig that," he said smiling. "The lil hoe hit me with five stacks right. I told the bitch, 'I know this ain't everything cause it's too even.'"

Keyshawn was looking puzzled. "Listen man, anytime a hoe hit you with some even money, you know the bitch stashing on you, pimp buddy."

"Oh, okay."

"Especially if she claiming that's its all the money she's got."

"So, what she say after you told her that?"

"What could the bitch say? I told her I'd be by to get the rest today. See another thing you gotta instill in 'em is to get used to paying you, lil dawg. And always, always put a bitch in the rear out the gate even before you touch 'em sexually, that's rule number one, Key."

"I feel you," Keyshawn said, feeling enlighten.

"I got to jump in this shower. You welcome to stay if you wanna."

"Nawh, I need to get going."

"Aight, I'ma have that for you in a minute."

* * * * *

Driving in the car, he thought about Quesha so he called her. "Hey, what's up?"

"Nothing, I see you a busy man, huh."

"Just tryna' get a few things together; that's all." "I know how it is," she said with a sigh.

"What you doing now? Can I come see you?"

"I don't know, what I tell you yesterday?"

"All that shit gone, I burned it up."

She was laughing. "Okay in that case, come on." She gave him her address before they hung up.

* * * * *

Quesha lived a few blocks away from where they'd met. He couldn't help but to notice the condition the outside of her house was in. Half the siding was missing off the front. The paint on the porch was chipped badly. There was a basement window knocked completely out and the dirt where the grass once was tracked everywhere as if kids used her front yard as the playground.

He completely disregarded all of that once she came out the door. Quesha emerged looking like a young ghetto diva wearing a skin tight, one piece Apple Bottom blue jean short outfit as she strolled up to the car smiling. He couldn't help but to think of what she must look like in her birthday suit.

"Oh, you switched cars too I see." He was in a bit of a trace.

"Huh, all yeah, switch cars, yeah."

"You alright?" she said laughing a little.

"I'm cool, I was just thinking about something," he said with a dumb look.

Thinking about the conversation he'd just had with T.A., he was back to himself.

"Can you leave?"

"I don't know, that depends on where we going."

"Nawh, I just wanted to ride and talk," he said, knowing what she was probably thinking.

"Oh, yeah we can do that," she said loosening back up.

During their brief drive though the city that ended at Washington Park, he learned that she was staying with a friend. She worked at a department store downtown and was saving money to get her own place. When asked about her family, Quesha was a bit reluctant to talk about them; he found this odd, but didn't want to pry.

They'd been walking along side a pond on a trail. She wanted to sit for a second, so they found a picnic table close by.

"Why were you in Mississippi so long?"

"My mother wanted me down there for a while to get away from here."

"Oh, you musta' been a bad boy, huh?" she said smiling.

"You can say that I guess."

"So, what's it like down there?" she inquired.

He told her about his experiences being in the South. He explained the difference in the people that lived there as opposed to Milwaukee natives. They talked about his grandmother and other family members he had in McComb. He loved his grandmother and was starting to miss her already. She had no companion; after his grandfather died, she never remarried. Sometimes Keyshawn could see how much she missed having his grandfather around. She would talk to him for hours about his grandfather, showing him pictures and telling

stories about the civil rights movement. They were
both very much a part of it and all of this was
intriguing to Keyshawn. He loved the story
actually. Quesha was moved by the strong sense of
love he had for his grandmother. She had never
had the chance to know any of her grandparents.
She barely knew her parents. Thus, explaining her
unwillingness to discuss her family, not that she
was embarrassed, but growing up in different
foster homes over the years, she'd seen her fair
share of abuse and neglect. Things that she cared
not to discuss and did her best to forget.

After talking for a while, they enjoyed ice cream
on the way back to her house. She thought that
Keyshawn was really nice. He was respectful,
courteous, and this was actually the first time she
shared an afternoon with anyone like this. She
definitely wanted to see him again and whatever
this cologne was that he was sporting made her
want to jump all over this nigga.

They were in front of her house now.

"So, what you doing later on?" she said, hoping
he would be free.

"I don't know right now, why what's up?"

"Oh, well just call me then."

Truth was he knew what he would be doing,
"her" if he wanted to, he was thinking as she got
out.

* * * * *

When he called Quesha later on that night, she informed him that she was washing clothes and he was welcome to come by. When he went over, she answered the door wearing jogging shorts and a tank top. As he walked behind her up the stairs, he couldn't help but notice the way her juicy ass was bouncing freely, with no panties on, it was just all over the place!

"My friend is out of town, you can have a seat in there," she said, pointing to the living room.

The inside was much nicer than outside. It was well kept and orderly so he didn't feel the least bit uncomfortable. She came back from the basement carrying a basket of clothes.

"You can come in here."

They sat on the bed laughing at comedians on *Mad TV* while she folded clothes.

When Quesha finished, she put on an Avant CD, then slid next to him to take his shirt off. She wasn't shy one bit. She pulled his dick out and stated sucking it like she was competing for a million-dollar prize, making sure that she devoured every inch, taking deep long strokes. By now, he was ready to have his way with Ms. Quesha and when she flipped over and exposed the spread and span of her ass, he couldn't believe what he was seeing. She was hot and when he pulled up behind her he could tell as she grabbed his dick to put it in herself. She was an animal. Wanting it in every possible position, he was no match for this one.

When he finally burned out, she rode and sucked it 'til it was nothing left. They both fell out and slept 'til morning.

Chapter 6

Milwaukee winters were brutal; so much so that it made Keyshawn almost wish he was back in McComb. It had been nearly six months since he'd been back and the future couldn't have looked brighter. T.A. had been well informed; the city was now seeing the effects of a serious drought. But they had an endless supply coming in monthly; the Mexicans could barely keep up with T.A. and Keyshawn. They had to make arrangements for monthly drop offs of 500 pounds or better depending on the last month's consumption. Through Brandon and his people, they were able to move well over half of these shipments every month. Brandon's network had expanded far beyond Milwaukee. He'd gone far north as Stevens Point when he heard that they were feeling the effects of the drought much worse than Milwaukee was. The arrangement they had was perfect. Everybody were eating well and nobody was complaining. They were all happy to be the ones with one of the few plugs in the city at a time like this.

Keyshawn was able to move his mother out of the projects and into another home in a pleasant neighborhood. She was back working now at Harley Davidson assembling motorcycles.

Keysha was loving life at Marquette as a freshman. She enjoyed the constant weekend parties that many of the young college students frequented there.

Red had recently moved to Chicago. His top earner had managed to establish an extremely lucrative clientele bringing in $1,500 a night on average. And the rest of his stable was trying their best to keep up.

* * * * *

The black Cadillac Escalade sat in front of the Amtrak train station running for about a half an hour. Keyshawn looked to check the time. He could barely see the hands on the watch, let alone the time; the face was completely embedded in high quality VVS diamonds. He turned on the interior light to get a better look.

"Where the fuck is this girl at?" he was speaking to himself out loud. Just as he turned the light out, two females came walking out of the station. They were both wrestling with luggage as they tried not to fall walking through snow. He unlocked doors. Quesha jumped in the front seat after putting her bag in the back.

"Damn, baby, I shoulda stayed in South Carolina. I can't stand this snow," she said, kissing him on the cheek.

"Who is this dame in my back seat?"

"Oh, that's the surprise I was telling you about; daddy, this is Venus, baby," she said smiling.

"Happy Birthday!!" It was Keyshawn's nineteenth birthday today.

"Say happy birthday to your new daddy, bitch," Quesha said, looking in the back seat.

"Happy Birthday, daddy," she said, leaning up to kiss him on the cheek. He stopped her in mid-air.

"Hold on, baby, you coming in this shit all wrong," he said mugging.

She pulled a roll of cash out of her bra and handed it to him. "I'm sorry, baby...now can I give you yo' birthday kiss?"

He toyed with the roll in both hands. "You sure can."

This made her the happiest hooker on the planet. She kissed him and was immediately turned on by the Givenchy cologne. When she sat back in her seat, Quesha handed him a Crown Royal bag stuffed with rolls of various sizes. *What a way to bring in your birthday. Damn this shit feels good*, he was thinking as he pulled off from the curb.

T.A. and Red were throwing him a party at Elite, a nightclub downtown. Before going to the party he took the girls home to freshen up. They both took showers and got dressed in all black to match what their pimp was wearing.

When they were in the truck and on their way, he looked at Quesha…just as fine as can be. Then thought about how things had changed between them over the past few months. At first, she was just a late night party for him after long hours of hustling. But that all changed one night when him and T.A. went to pick up one of T.A. hoes from a gig she did at a bachelor party. T.A.'s bitch came walking out of the hotel talking with Quesha. Keyshawn spotted her and rolled down the window calling her real name. She almost went into a near panic when she turned her head to see Keyshawn looking her square in the face. She hurried off to get in the car with some nigga, whom he later on found out through T.A., was a half-ass tennis shoe pimp. He rolled the window back up with a million thoughts running through his mind.

"Who was that bitch you were talking to?" T.A. said looking at his hoe Kitty through the rear view mirror.

"That was this bitch, Luscious," she said, handing him her purse.

Luscious, what the hell! Keyshawn was thinking to himself.

T.A. just looked at him curiously. Once he dropped Kitty off, he asked Keyshawn what was going on with him and that bitch. Keyshawn reluctantly told him that he had been tricking off his dick with her for the past month and a half.

After T.A. scolded him for doing the number one thing that a player didn't do, as he said. He then started giving him some insight how to flip the script on the bitch and put her down. Keyshawn felt like a complete idiot. Here he was rendezvousing with the bitch for free and she was breaking with some chump who was riding around in a Cadillac hooptie. Stupid wasn't the word and he understood why T. A. was looking at him shaking his head.

All the nights she would fuck him to sleep, he always wondered how a chick so young was so experience sexually. Now he knew, and he had a trick for the bitch. He called her later that night and got no answer. She called him back the next morning.

"Hey, what's up?" she said dryly.

"Don't *what's up* me now, bitch...you didn't have a word for me last night," he said feeling dumb.

"Well, you seen that I was with somebody. I just didn't wanna be disrespectful."

He was steaming, but remembered T.A.'s advice to play it cool. So he calmed down.

"So, what happened, I thought you worked at a store downtown."

"Well, now you know I lied. Look...I really do apologize. But I got to be honest, it's not like you my man or anything."

At this point he was feeling like a super sucka.

"So, was that yo' pimp?"

"Nawh, I pay that nigga what I want for taking me places and being my security," she said chuckling.

T.A.'s words were echoing though his mind now, "Once the bitch establishes that the nigga ain't pimping, go in the paint hard on her. If she rejects it what you got to lose – nothing; at least you won't be going on fucking a hoe for free anymore, my nigga."

"Bitch, I ain't no sucka and if you wanna continue fucking with me you gotta start pushing some cash my way hoe."

Quesha was stunned, but she was also relieved that her secret finally became visible to Keyshawn. And when he finished spitting that script, she was smiling on the inside.

"Okay, well, come get yo' money then, daddy," she said proudly. From there on out, it was pimping ever since. * * * * *

They arrived to the party just around 11:00 p.m. He stepped out of the Escalade and when his black gators hit the ground, he felt the crisp cold air flowing off of Lake Michigan. He zipped up the black mink and as they made their way through the VIP line, every bitch instantly became jealous – especially the squares.

"Girl, you see them two silly looking bitches? He must be their pimp," the chick said.

"Yeah, must be," said her buddy, all the while thinking, *that nigga can be my pimp any day*, as she smiled to herself.

When Keyshawn made it through the door, he immediately became the center of attention. Red was the first to notice him. He came over and saluted his comrade.

"Happy Birthday, nigga."

Red was wearing a Salvatore Ferragamo number with matching red Mauri's.

"Thanks, fam."

They walked to the VIP where most of the invited guests were. T.A. was conversing with Bone and Fat Boy when they came in.

"What's up, baby? Happy Birthday!" T.A. said, rushing over toward Keyshawn.

The VIP was decked in white Italian leather; its walls were covered in black silk screened wall paper and the entire area was big enough to accommodate about a hundred guests comfortably. Most of the guests were pimps, hustlers, and an assortment of niggas whom they did business with.

Every chick in the club was striving to make their way to the area, as they crowded the doorway looking for a familiar face that might've been able to assist them in gaining access to the privileged area.

T.A. and Keyshawn were off to the side.

"You looking good homie," he said, admiring Keyshawn's attire.

"Thanks, where you get that suit from? It's slick as hell," Keyshawn responded.

"One of my hoes knocked for some plastic, so me and the bitch went on a shopping spree," he said looking at his suit. This nigga loved white and he too made sure his hoes were color coordinated with him.

"You got a new project you working on, huh?" T.A. said, referring to Venus.

"Yeah, pimp...a fresh addition to Camp Key. My bitch brought her back from Myrtle Beach, South Carolina. She said the bitch was down with some nigga that was playing and took his eyes off the bitch one too many times."

"Wow, did you call the nigga and serve him the bad news?"

"Nawh, not yet. I just scooped the hoes up and I ain't even had time to process the bitch all the way in yet." Just then Bone walked up.

"Say, mane...these hoes going crazy tryna' get back here. Some bitch just grabbed my arm and damn near pulled it out the socket. I think we need to get some hoe repellant by that door."

They all laughed as he walked away.

"You know what though pimping?" T.A. said, putting his arm on Keyshawn's shoulder. "I'm proud of you; you went to pimping on that lil bitch and ain't stopped. You know why hoes pay players? Cause we got enough sense to ask for some money and stand on it, baby. Make sure when a hoe see you that you always at your best. Don't let a bitch catch you off balance and don't ever let 'em see you sweat. You gotta build a strong name for yourself with these hoes and keep it that way 'til you die. Cause real hoes...they don't choose a nigga on how much money he got. They're going off the caliber of a pimp's game along with his stats. They want a pimp who can take their hoeing to the next level. Always remember that, homie."

Red waved them over to the picture area, they took a few flicks before Red grabbed the mic and summons everybody to the center of the room for a toast.

"I wanna say happy birthday to my brother Key. The coldest young nigga coming outta the Mil, next to me that is," he said laughing. "Seriously, I want you hoes to get a good look at this nigga cause y'all gone be seeing a lot more of him," he said, raising his glass. Keyshawn was standing next to Red with Quesha and Venus beaming behind him. There would be no stopping him now. He had a stomp down hoe along with a fresh new prospect. His hustle was the strongest out of any young nigga in Milwaukee. And he had a real nigga with plenty of product and muscle behind 'em. *What better formula for success!!*

Chapter 7

Keyshawn rarely slept after 12:00 p.m. but last night had been never ending. He didn't get to bed until well after 5:00 a.m. and when he finally woke up, he had the worst headache he'd ever experienced. He wasn't a drinker, but since it was his birthday, he figured what the hell. He noticed that Quesha was already up, she wasn't in the bed and the rest of the townhouse was quiet.

When he finally forced himself out of bed, he headed straight for the medicine cabinet for some aspirin, and then poured a glass of 7UP in an attempt to settle his stomach from the hangover.

As he began thinking to himself, *I'm never doing that shit again*, Quesha and Venus were coming through the door.

"You alright, baby?" Quesha said smiling. He just looked at her.

"You was fucked up last night, daddy," she said, sitting next to him on the couch, rubbing his head. Not knowing what to do, Venus just stood near the door.

"Why you just standing there looking stupid in shit, bitch...sit down or something," he said. Key hated for this new bitch to see him off his square, especially this early in the game.

She went over to the loveseat and sat staring at the TV

"Where y'all coming from?"

Quesha was massaging his temples as she sat on his lap facing him.

"We went to the grocery store for breakfast food," she said, looking back at Venus gesturing for her to come over and assist her in the pampering of their pimp. She took off her coat and walked around the sofa to rub his shoulders.

"Good, cause I'm so hungry I could eat one of you hoes right now."

Knowing that was a joke, they all began laughing.

This made Venus more comfortable; she'd barely known Quesha a few weeks and had yet to spend a full twenty-four hours with Key. Even though she knew it was pimping, she still felt like she was intruding. But this was natural for a new comer to any pimp's stable.

They catered to Key until he realized he hadn't brushed his teeth or freshened up yet. As he made his way to the shower, the girls headed to the kitchen to prepare a late breakfast.

After a long, hot shower, he emerged feeling much better. When he came out of the bathroom, he put on a blue silk robe Quesha had brought back for him as a gift.

"You know, baby…that robe looks a lot better with you in it," she said, putting a plate of food on the table in the living room.

MOTIVATION: MASTERING THE GAME

This bitch always knows the right thing to say, he was thinking while flipping through the cable stations.

The *Travel Channel* was doing a segment on New Orleans; they were advertising the upcoming Mardi Gras. The host was talking to the mayor who said that they were expecting over a million tourists during the next two weeks.

"It's gone be a lot of money down there, daddy. Can we go check it out?" Quesha said, as they took turns feeding him his breakfast. Venus was holding the plate of cooked food, while Quesha served him fruit off of another.

"We might just do that; I need to get away for a minute."

Plus, it would give him a chance to see firsthand what this bitch, Venus, was really made of.

Once he finished, it was time to get dressed; he had to meet Brandon so they could square away some business. Venus was with him, they needed to get better acquainted and it was time to start his grooming process.

They went to a house he used for storage and transactions. As he waited for B, he started with questions about who she was and her background. She told him that she was eighteen and was from Charlotte, North Carolina, but hadn't been there since she was sixteen. She'd been with a pimp who went by the name, Finesse for the past year. She met him on a track in Myrtle Beach; he was a terrible pimp who managed her money poorly. She eventually discovered that he was a crackhead when she caught him smoking the pipe in their hotel room. She'd been trying to get away from him, and then she met Quesha who began telling her about Key. After Quesha told her how they were

living, she was ready to leave with her.

Once Key had finished screening her, he decided that this nigga, Finesse, was no P; thus, deeming him unworthy of a real pimp's phone call. But on the other hand...what if this bitch was lying. One thing he wasn't was green, and he knew that if a bitch thought she could pull it off, she'd lie in a heartbeat. He learned this from a few incidents with Quesha; yes...hoes lied for a living and sometimes their pimp was no exception to that rule.

The call to Finesse wasn't pleasant; when he told the nigga that he had his ex-bitch in custody, he could feel this dude's heartbeat drop through the phone. Young Key hadn't experienced this part of the game yet, but he knew it couldn't have been sweet. And he was right, losing a hoe to another pimp (whatever the reason) was a disturbing blow to any mack.

"I don't know who you are player, but you ain't got my bitch. If you do, put the hoe on the phone and let her make a disclaimer on a pimp her damn self," Finesse said. His biggest fear had come true. After she didn't check in at the room a week ago, he didn't wanna think about it, but he knew she was gone. This was the only bitch that he had managed to hold on to for as long as he did in the last few years of his career. He may never knock a decent enough hoe to support his habit and keep him with enough money for at least a room every night. *No he needed to talk to her!* He was thinking, as the panic was getting heavier by the second.

"So, you gone put the bitch on the phone or are you gone keep acting as a spokesman for this hoe?" Key could hear the desperation in his voice. He figured there was no

MOTIVATION: MASTERING THE GAME

harm in letting her tell him herself. She had already chosen up. He handed her the phone.

"Tell this dude what's happening."

As soon as she said, "hello" he could hear him on the other end cursing and calling her every hoe in the book.

"I ain't fucking with you no more, I'm wit Key now," she said, and then handed the phone back to Key.

"You satisfied, player?"

"Fuck you, nigga," he said as he hung up the phone. Finesse had no class mixed with poor sportsmanship and the game had no room for either if you wanted to be the best. Something Key heard T.A. express to a few pimps over the phone during a serving call.

Brandon had made it there by now. They did what they had to do and everybody left.

On the way back, he talked about his expectations, made her aware of the penalties for meddling with other pimps and staying in pocket at all times. She sat

82

quietly, taking it all in. Most of it was familiar dialogue as some things were standard amongst pimps and hoes. But it was protocol, and would become a ritual each time he knocked fresh work.

* * * * *

A few days later, after handling all of his affairs, they set off for New Orleans. He phoned Red to see if he might meet him there and he assured him that he would; T.A. was busy dispatching his people through the website he had built. His hoes had clients as far away as Canada and Europe. So there was no need for him to take it to the roads.

Chapter 8

The weather in New Orleans was fairly mild this time of year. It was a far cry from Milwaukee's snow storms and blizzards. Tourist from all over the world booked hotels throughout the city and surrounding parishes. The streets near the French Quarters were filled with vacationers and locals from various walks of life who were there merely to enjoy the festivities and parades of this yearly event.

But the streets of Canal and Bourbon, which were the center of it all, also attracted a darker element. Dope pushers operated in the bathrooms of bars, thieves lurked the crowded streets in search of prey, while hookers mixed and mingled looking to catch the eye of a trick. Bourbon Street welcomed any legitimate business dealing in the area of sex. From sex stores to peep shows; strip joints to massage parlors; it was a whore's dream and a pimp's cream. Players from all around the country were in attendance turning hotel rooms into workstations where whores could carry out their duties. Key and Red arrived a couple of days early, enthused about collecting their rations. The day they arrived, they wasted no time. The girls gathered themselves and dressed to hit the streets.

Red had a quick pep-talk with his people before releasing them to the field.

"Cash, plastic, diamonds and furs," he said as the three chicks: Apple, Sunshine, and Cinnamon got out of the car.

Key instructed his hoes to target more whites instead of black ones; especially Venus because she was light skinned and slender with big titties—a combination of features that white men loved.

While the hoes were working, they figured they'd cruise the area and stop at a few joints in hopes of stealing one of these niggas' bitches. A pimp's work is never done and staying in pursuit of a new bitch was a must.

After riding for a minute, they realized that to be more effective, they needed to be on the concrete where all the action was. They were pressing any hoe that looked like she wanted a new home. One even took Key's card and said she'd call him later. Even after indicating that she had a pimp, whoever he was he was slipping and Key was ready to let him know just how much.

"Call me when you ready to jump that sucka," he said, walking off.

A couple of hours later, they found themselves at a strip club on Bourbon. Inside, Red recognized a pimp he knew from Milwaukee. His name was Smoove. He was an old school player who was known for being brutal with his bitches. When they would disobey him, he would administer some nasty beatings that sometimes took months to heal. Smoove's philosophy behind this was once another bitch saw what happen to a fellow *wife-inlaw* for getting out of order, she would think twice about pulling the same shit and he would make sure that his other hoes were front and center to witness the horror. But as long as they didn't get out of line, he was always the perfect gentleman.

Smoove was happy to see some cat's he knew from the Mil, he was always on the road and didn't see many familiar faces. So when he did, it was always a pleasure. He and Red were reminiscing about the last time they'd seen each other in Detroit on the track. Smoove had a bitch named Passion, but everybody that knew her best called her Fingers because she was one hell of a thief. She'd pull a trick's pants down to give him a blow job and would be taking his wallet out of his back pocket at the same time. By the time he'd realized it was gone, she'd be somewhere else pulling the same move on her next victim. Robbery wasn't beneath Fingers either. If she couldn't get it out of them that way; depending on how big he was, she'd crack him over the head with something and straight take his shit. The bitch was a pure beast and wasn't scared of anything; every pimp on the streets wanted to have a run with the hoe. She kept the nigga Smoove in big name shit. Big watches, rings, necklaces—you name it, she stole it.

But one night, all this caught up with her and she nearly lost her life. She had dated a cat that was balling in D-town. He was drunk and fell asleep in the hotel room. When he woke up, all his jewels were gone along with his money. The jewels alone were rumored to be worth over $40,000 and the cash was well over ten Gs.

Turns out, that this nigga wasn't just ballin', but he was the man in Detroit. By morning, word was all over the streets that there was a reward out for anyone who apprehended the bitch and brought her to him alive. He also had a handful of local dirty cops on his payroll that had done nearly everything under the sun short of killing somebody for this nigga. Smoove hadn't had the chance to get her safely out of town. He knew that a lick this big could get her killed, so he didn't send her back to work that night and planned on leaving after they got up first thing in the morning. Well, by the time they were up, so were all these other muthafuckas looking to get the reward. Those dirty cops had been on the prowl early shaking down everybody who they thought may have had a connection to the chick.

They started with the local pimps, and after they busted down the door of a nigga named World, they came out with the information they were looking for. World had told them that he believed it was a bitch that messed with a pimp out of Milwaukee (The pimp world is a small one and everybody who's somebody knows the major players). He gave them the names Smoove and Passion and the description of Smoove's Mercedes Benz. Once they had the description of the car, they split up in separate directions and started searching all the hotels where they thought they might have been staying. The search was proving to be pointless, and then by noon, one of them spotted a green Mercedes with Wisconsin plates at the Courtyard Marriot. He immediately notified the others and they were there within minutes. They sat in the parking lot for not even a half an hour before the two people they were looking for came strolling up to the vehicle. Before they could get in, the cops were all over them. After a search of their bag, they found jewels and cash in the trunk of the Benz.

They separated them into two cars; one with her and the stolen property and the other with Smoove with just him and three cops inside. They took her to collect the reward, when they got there, they didn't know what this nigga had planned for her and didn't care. All they wanted was the $50,000 he had promised for her capture. He took the jewels and let them keep the cash. Then he handed the reward money over to them in a bag as the officers walked away shaking their heads. She knew what was about to happen to her as they slammed her down violently on to a bed.

They all took turns raping and sodomizing her for six hours before beating her and slashing her face. Then finally, when they were done, they had the officers drive Smoove over to them so they could dump her body in the back of his Benz.

"You betta' watch who yo' hoe stealing from around here, nigga, this ain't Milwaukee. Now get this bitch out of here while you got the chance," World said.

At first, Smoove thought she was dead until she started moving. When he drove her to the hospital, the police were sweating him like he did it. But what was he supposed to tell them, that their own people let this happen? He just told them he found her in an alley near the track. She was in the hospital for four months recovering from her injuries.

The first thing she said to Smoove when she able to talk was, "We shoulda' left town that night, at least we still would've had the shit that I took."

He couldn't believe this bitch, here she was damn near dead, and all she could think about was losing the shit she stole. When he finished telling Red and Key the story, Red said, "Now that's a diehard hoe for you."

Key was shaking his head. "Where she at now?"

Smoove put his drink down firmly. "Where you think the bitch at, down here somewhere getting a pimp some money," they all laughed their asses off.

"Man you ice wit' this shit, baby," Red said, breaking the laughter.

"Just another day at the office, that's why you young niggas better go to State Farm and put some insurance on ya' hoes."

They thought he was just talking out the side of his neck, but Smoove meant every word of what he just said. He was an old vet and these young cats were mere puppies. He had seen everything that could be seen in the pimp game and understood that pimping and hoeing were amongst the most dangerous occupations in the streets. Most people just saw the glitz and glamour. But Smoove had seen many good players and bitches die in the mist of this shit.

Red was fixing his mouth to say something when his phone rang. He looked at the caller ID, it was Apple. He went to the restroom to answer it.

"Yeah," he said, hoping she was calling to report a bankroll.

"The police got Sunshine and Cinnamon," she said sounding nervous. He couldn't believe what he was hearing.

"Where you at?"

She told him where she was and he instructed her to meet him at a nearby corner on Canal.

When he came out the bathroom, Key and Smoove were talking. Smoove was telling him about a few hot spots in the country.

"Man, that was one of my bitches; she said the other two got knocked by the law. Can you believe that shit? Not even a full day and I'm already out of bail money."

"You know how this shit go pimpin', sometimes a pimp gotta pay to play too; right?"

"Yeah, I can dig that, but I'll be right back. I'm 'bout to go meet this bitch and see what happened."

"Aight," Key said as Red walked away. While they were talking, Key got a call from Quesha; she was telling him that he needed to come get some of his money. He and Smoove left the club and when they got down the block, one of Smoove's hoes was walking across the street, so he went over there to get an update on his trap as well. Key told Quesha to meet him at McDonald's on Canal. When he arrived, she and Venus were both there. They all went outside and got in the Escalade. Both of them handed over his trap and got back on the grind.

When he caught up with Red, he told him that his people had been picked up on suspicion of prostitution based on the way that they were dressed. Apple wasn't really dressed all that provocative and this is why he believes she wasn't sweated.

They were back on Bourbon now, and Red was giving Smoove the spill on what happened to his people. Smoove informed him on the procedure that the N.O.P.D. would take each time they saw one of the two hoes anywhere near the track; they would lock them up every time and he advised Red to start looking at another area such as the Casino which wasn't far away or few clubs near Chef Highway. Red was pissed and Key would make a note to have his hoes tone their dress code down a little bit more to prevent this from happening to him.

The next day, Red had his hoes back. He left Apple on the blade and put the other two down near the casino. He wasn't with that club shit; he liked his hoes to constantly be moving.

Key had a good night and saw no need to disturb his groove. Venus was most impressive, she racked in $800 while Quesha only $600. Back at the hotel, he could see the competiveness starting to brew between the two of them. He was loving every minute of it, it hadn't got nasty yet. But he caught Quesha eyeing Venus jealously as he was counting the money that night and he purposely separated both of their earnings on the table as he counted. He did this as somewhat of a reward ceremony for Venus and a quiet scolding for Quesha. It worked because today they were both busting their asses like crazy. Venus was tryna' maintain her title and Quesha was trying to reclaim her position as front runner.

At about one o'clock that morning, Venus was calling him, requesting to be picked up at a hotel near the Super Dome. When he pulled up, she was beaming like a Christmas tree.

"Here you go, daddy" she said as she handed him a stack of bills all fifties and hundred dollar bills. He was folding the cash to put it in his pocket when she put the Rolex in his lap. He pulled off.

"What the hell you do, tie somebody up to get all this shit?" he said bewildered.

"Nawh, I put him to sleep."

He'd almost forgotten about the sleeping agent he gave her before they left Milwaukee.

"You didn't kill him did you?"

That was the last thing a pimp needed.

"No, I just gave him a lil bit; he was breathing when I left, daddy; don't worry."

For the rest of the way to the hotel, she told him what happened. She met the trick at a bar in a hotel on Canal. He was tipsy and she noticed that he had a lot of money when he was paying for his drinks. When he approached her, she then noticed the watch. They talked for a lil bit before he asked her to go to his room with him. Once they got in the room, he poured himself another drink before going to the bathroom. She quickly got out the agent and slipped some in the glass. While she was doing this, he was coming out the bathroom. She got nervous and dropped the rest on the floor by accident. Once he drunk the potion, he was out in less than twenty minutes. Then she immediately went for his pockets where she found the wallet and a key to the safe in the hotel room. She opened the safe and found the rest of the money and after she took the watch, she headed out the side door of the hotel.

When she finished telling the story, Venus was smiling from ear to ear. Key and Red were in the front seat digging how she operated so swiftly. *And to think she was the new comer.*

They got to the hotel and Key walked her in. While riding in the truck listening to her story, he couldn't help but think about the story Smoove had told him the day before. He decided to retire her for the night and maybe even tomorrow. Once they got in the room, he examined the watch more closely. It was definitely authentic, solid gold with an orange dial that had rubies and emeralds in it. Yeah, this bitch did well alright; over $3,000 cash and a Rolex that had to be worth at least ten large in one night awarded the hoe the right to turn it in early.

At about 3:00 a.m. Key and Quesha came back to the room. Venus was all showered up lying across the bed, watching a movie, eating popcorn and some other snacks.

"Hey, y'all," she said as they came in, all the while smiling slyly at Quesha.

Quesha was thinking to herself. *What the hell is the bitch doing in here chilling and I'm out humping 'til three o'clock in the morning?* She had made well over a thousand today and just knew that this bitch couldn't have topped that. But she soon realized that she was dead wrong as Key went to do his daily count once again. She took one look at the Rolex and the stack of money and nearly slammed the door as she went in the bathroom to take a hot bath. It took everything in Venus' body to stop her from laughing. Even Key nearly cracked up himself. But he knew better, to do so would have been a direct blow below the belt and he wanted to keep his game clean. Plus, this bitch Venus was just catching up, Quesha had been bringing him stacks of money every since he first put her down.

Chapter 9

When the phone started ringing it wouldn't stop. After the first round, the caller was calling again. He didn't get to bed until nearly 4:00 a.m. and here was somebody pestering him five hours later. Key was tired, but when he looked at the caller ID and saw that it was Keysha, he knew that it had to be important for her to be calling him this early. He flipped the phone open.

"Hello."

"What's up, bro? Where you at?"

"I'm outta town, why what's up?"

"The police took Brandon to jail last night; he had some of that stuff on him."

He was awake now.

"How much?"

"I think he said twenty pounds. Is that a lot?"

"Hell, yeah that's a lot, it's enough. When did you talk to him?"

"This morning," she said, starting to cry. "They gone send him to jail ain't they?"

"I don't know."

But he knew that Brandon was dog meat. Twenty pounds would send Jesse Jackson to jail.

"Did he get a bail yet?" he said, rubbing his eyes.

"No, he said he ain't been to court. They told him it could take up to a week for that," she was sad.

"Well, ain't nothing we can do until then, just go see him and find out what happened. And make sure you tell him not to be discussing his case on them jail phones or with any of them niggas in there. I'ma call T.A. and have him go get B a lawyer. He'll be alright. I'll call you later on when I get up sis."

"Okay."

After she hung up she felt a little better. Keysha felt like it was her fault because she was the one who introduced him to Keyshawn. Feeling terrible, she laid on the bed wiping away tears as she waited for Brandon to call her back.

When he closed his phone Keyshawn couldn't think about anything at the time except for a few more hours of sleep. He would deal with this matter as soon as he woke back up.

A few hours later, he was awake. The first thing he did was call T.A.; he told him what happened and T.A. got a lawyer down to see Brandon at the county jail right away.

T.A kept high-powered lawyers on retainer because he knew that he could need one at anytime. The attorneys he had didn't mind taking illicit funds. And they were well connected, making them very effective in court.

Two hours after the lawyer went to see Brandon, he was in intake court and free on bond immediately following the hearing.

Brandon was at home with Keysha when he called Key. He told him that the police had pulled him over on a routine traffic stop. They asked for permission to search the car and he told them no, they then brought a dog, who got a hit near the trunk of the vehicle. This was enough for them to request a search warrant. The warrant was granted and when they went through the trunk they found the pounds in plain view.

When they got him to the station, narcotics questioned him, wanting to know where he got the weed from, but after a few minutes, Brandon requested to speak with a lawyer. After he requested a lawyer for the fourth time, they finally left him alone and transported him to the county jail.

Key knew the boys would try to get B to rat, but he passed the test and didn't give them shit.

"Alright, homie, I'll holla at you when I get back in town."

When they were getting ready for work, Quesha was dragging her ass purposely, something that she'd never done before. Key knew the type of stunt she was trying to pull and he wasn't about to have it. He went to the bathroom were she was doing her hair.

"What the fucks taking you so long to get the fuck up out of here?"

"Nothing, I'm doing my hair."

"Don't play with me, bitch…you been doing your hair for an hour and a half, it ain't never took you this long. Hurry up and get the fuck up outta here before you find these Prada's up yo' black ass."

When they were loading up in the truck, Quesha sat in the backseat.

"You don't wanna get up there, girl?" Venus said standing outside the door.

"Nawh, you King Hoe around here now, you get up there."

"Girl, you trippin," she said as she got in the front seat.

The atmosphere was tense and quiet as Key pushed the truck though the gritty streets. When they arrived, he was about to go through his *Daily Motivational Spill* as he called it, but Quesha cut him off.

"Yeah, we know, don't bring back no less than…" before she could get it out, he backed handed her across the face and busted her lip.

"Bitch don't ever interrupt me when I'm talking."

Scared, Venus said, "Can I get out, daddy?"

"Yeah, go ahead."

He was still looking at Quesha when Venus got out. A tear rolled down her face, this was the first time he had to physically discipline her and her feelings were hurt.

What the fuck is this bitch's problem? Key thought to himself. But he knew what it was, another bitch had come into the picture and out shinned her. She was wishing she hadn't brought the hoe, Venus, back home with her now.

"You mad about this hoe getting a pimp some money, bitch? Stop worry about what this whore's doing and take care of your business. You a better hoe than this," he said, trying to get her fired up. The fact of the matter was, Venus had just caught some good luck running into that trick last night. She had just happened to be at the right place at the right time.

"I'ma do better, but you ain't have to hit me in front of that bitch."

"Get yo' ass out and go get some fuckin' money. And if you get outta pocket like that again, I might make her beat your fucking ass," he had a stone face when he said it. No way was Key about to let his emotions override his intellect. Sure she'd been with him from the start, but that gave her no special privileges – she would adhere to the same rules and regulations as Venus did.

Later that day, he was telling Red about the situation and where all the competiveness between his hoes was leading to.

"She's jealous P., that shit is common when a pimp starts fattening his stable up. You ain't seen the half of what that bitch is gone do if you don't hurry up and put her back in proper working order."

"But she brought the bitch to me though."

"I know she did, man. But you gotta understand that a hoe ain't no different than any other woman. They have feelings and can sometimes be territorial too, my nigga." It takes a special bitch to fully accept a nigga's pimping. And right now is her test; see you didn't have this problem before because she was the only hoe you had. And she's not just acting like that because the lil hoe out did her for a couple of days, she's showing signs of jealousy pimpin'. Believe me, I been through that same shit. Get that bitch back on track before that shit starts affecting your pockets, baby."

Red's words were the truth, and Key knew it. He made a mental note to take care of it.

While they were riding, Red told him that he'd heard the police had nabbed Smoove, but he wasn't sure of the charge. He also said that he was on the hunt for the bitch, Passion, or any other hoe that the nigga had down there on the loose.

"The name of the game is smash on a bitch and ain't no friends in this shit."

Apple happened to be the strongest link out of the three hoes that Red brought with him. She was under strict orders to press any one of Smoove's people that she encountered on the blade.

It didn't take Apple long to spot one. She saw her going into a hotel with a trick and waited on her until she came back out. She came out about a half an hour later. And Apple was right on her heels.

"Hey baby, I see you working hard every day."

"What's up, I been seeing you too, Red yo' pimp, ain't he?"

"Yeah, I heard your pimp's in jail though; you know niggas can be rough on a bitch out here without a pimp, baby. I've even known of hoes with no representation to be kidnapped down here," Apple was lying.

But the bitch was green, Smoove only had her for a month and she was a fresh turn-out at eighteen.

"For real?" she said with a scared look on her face.

"Yeah, baby, you need to get with my daddy. Niggas down here know not to fuck with his hoes," she said lying again. Sure Red was a reputable young P., but the truth was that he only knew two pimps in New Orleans, Smoove and Key.

"I don't know...I got a daddy anyway."

"What good is he gone do you in jail. Come on now, baby...if you was in there think that nigga would be thinking about yo' ass. And I heard how he be trying to kill his hoes when they get out of line." When she said that, the lil chick stiffened up, she'd witnessed Smoove administer one of those beatings and vowed that she would never do anything wrong.

"What's your name anyway?" Apple said.

"Mercedes."

"I'm Apple, you wanna meet my daddy, he cool you can talk to him yourself," she said, knowing that if this bitch got anywhere near Red it was a wrap.

Red got the call as him and Key was eating at the buffet inside Casino Mirage.

"What's up, bitch?" he said, chewing on a piece of shrimp.

"I got somebody that wanna meet you, her name is

Mercedes."

This was music to this nigga's ears.

"Put the bitch on the phone."

They said a few words to one another before he told her to catch a cab to his hotel with Apple then hung up the phone.

"I told you nigga, my bitch don't play. That nigga's 'bout to be short a hoe. I need you to take me to my car, pimpin'."

Passion was turning the corner when she saw Mercedes and Apple hopping into a cab.

"Bitch, Smoove's gonna have your ass for this."

"Oh, she won't have to worry about that honey," Apple said with a smile as the taxi pulled off. Passion stood there for a second in disbelief.

Key rode around thinking about what to do with Quesha 'til he finally said, "fuck that bitch, I'ma keep on pimpin' and if she becomes too much of a problem, I'll fire her ass before I let her mess up my program," he shook it off and got back focused.

When he hit Canal Street he caught a glimpse of what appeared to be Passion. She went into a bar and he jumped in pursuit. It was her alright, as soon as he walked through the door, she was at the bar smoking a cigarette and ordering a drink.

"Mind if I sit here with you?" he said.

"Aye, that's your business, I don't own this place."

She was a tough bitch who wasn't that much of a looker close up, even without the scars that he assumed must have came from her accident in Detroit. But damn how she looked, if this broad was anything like what he heard, she would be just perfect as a new addition to his stable.

"Anyway, ain't you a pimp? Cause if you are, there's no sense in us even starting a conversation. I'm happy where I am, baby," she said, pulling on the square. "Plus, you too young; I don't think you even ready for a vet bitch like me." she said looking at him now.

"You know I'm a pimp, baby, and never mind my age. You looking to get a breath of fresh air, hoe. I can see it all in yo' face; you wanna try something better. You just too scared to act on it."

"The only fresh air I need is right outside this door," she said, getting up from the bar stool. She was loyal to the nigga Smoove, they had years in together and it would take more than a few days in jail for her to choose another pimp.

Key didn't sweat it; he'd catch her again and pop pimping at the bitch even harder next time.

Later that night, Venus called him to pick up some money. She also informed him that she had a bitch with her who wanted to talk to him. When he met them, the chick was acting really nervous.

"What's happenin', baby? You looking to upgrade I hear," he said, counting the money Venus gave him.

"Yeah, but I think Smoove will try to kill me if he finds out. Will he find out?"

"Will he find out?! I'm sure he will. I don't secretly pimp, hoe."

"Well, what if he tries to do something to me?"

"Look, baby...if you choosing, don't worry about all that. Let me deal with Smoove."

"Okay," she said. When she handed him the cash, her hand was shaking badly.

"Damn, bitch what you got Parkinson's or something? Hoe yo' hands shaking worse than Muhammad Ali's."

He took her to the room she was staying in to get her belongings, which she threw in the back of the truck.

After he dropped them off at work, Key called Red to do a little boasting.

"Yeah, P., you ain't the only one knocking hoes around here, I just bumped him for one myself," Red was laughing.

"Which one?"

"The bitch Classy, the one who always wearing that red wig."

"Oh, okay. Say man, that nigga betta' hurry up and get out fo' somebody have to donate a bitch to him."

They both laughed.

"Right, he'll be waiting for the pimp god to come see him cause we both know that ain't gonna happen."

At 4:00 a.m. Passion was up having a chat with the other girls Smoove had in his squad. She was attempting to put fear in them, in hopes that they wouldn't do like the other two, they didn't wait two full days of him being in jail before they fled.

"Them hoes gone pay for this shit, and I hope y'all ain't thinking of doing the same thing. I talked to daddy; he wants us to come see him tomorrow morning. Whatever happened to a bitch being loyal to her pimp?"

It was easy for her to say this; Passion had been with this nigga for years, but the other two hung around merely out of fear and nothing else.

"Y'all making the right choice because them other two hoes will be penalized."

Passion's speech hadn't worked, they both wanted to see when he was getting out so they knew how much time they had to stall before they ran themselves.

When they went to the jail that morning, Passion was the first to talk with him. They were in a booth talking through a three-inch thick glass window. Smoove appeared calm as always, even after Passion had told him what happened, he still never showed emotion or even looked as though he was affected by it. She told him about Red's hoe, Apple, knocking Mercedes and about the run in she had with Key. She wasn't sure where Classy was, she just knew that when she came back to the room all her bags were gone.

That part really pissed him off because Classy was the reason he was in jail in the first place. The day he was arrested, Smoove was chastising her in the car. She'd been working lazily and he'd gotten fed up with it. While he was in the process of handing down his punishment, the police pulled up. When they got him out of the car they found a gun on his waist. Then they found the cocaine that he had in his pocket for personal use. The drugs weren't a problem, but the State of Louisiana had strict gun laws and they were denying him bail until he had a preliminary arraignment, which wouldn't be for another two weeks.

He wanted to kill the bitch Classy, and he had a few ideas in store for Key and Red. Smoove knew the game was cop and blow. But he wasn't honoring a nigga knocking him in this fashion; plus, these were some young punks to him. He'd been in the game longer than they'd lived on earth. They would pay; he just hoped that they hung around long enough for him to get his chance.

He didn't convey any of this to Passion, when the guard told him that his time was up he simply told her bye and that he'd call her later. He didn't even address the other two, Smoove was much too seasoned not to see that they had already made up their minds to abscond. The whole purpose of telling Passion to bring them was so that he could read them, face to face.

And he was right; they were both gone by night fall. They'd packed their bags and left town out of fear of what he'd do to them if they got with another pimp and stayed in New Orleans.

Chapter 10

The two weeks that followed had been good to Key. So good, that he decided to stay after the festivals were over. Classy came into the family working like the Energizer Bunny. With the right understanding of the game, she was the kind of bitch that "let" a nigga pimp. Key liked this about her; he really didn't have to say too much to motivate Classy. She would be up, dressed, and ready to go before everybody. After they came in from work one morning, Venus made a comment about her wifein-law's work ethic.

"Daddy, this bitch acting like she trying to win the Hoe of The Year Award."

"The hoe keeps getting at my money the way she is, I might give the bitch a vacation or something," Key said jokingly. However, Classy was just the piece that he needed at the time. She sent two messages and they were both heard by Venus and Quesha. One was that she was happy with her hoein' and she was very much worth her weight in gold. The other stated that any bitch with a poor performance had no place in the family. This motivated Venus and woke up Quesha! Key was definitely loving this bitch, she made a pimp's job easy. In fact she was helping him pimp and didn't even know it.

* * * * *

Red was back at home in Chicago when he got the call from Smoove.

"Yo' sucka ass still in town, so I can collect that bitch and show you how a real pimp stand on a hoe," Smoove said.

"First of all nigga, you lost the bitch fair and square. But since you being tacky about losing the bitch, I don't need you to show me shit. That hoe's been paying a pimp quit well, more than you was getting out the bitch I'm sure," Red said laughing.

"You lil' pussy half ass pimp, that was a snake move; if you had guts, you wouldn't have had to wait 'til I was down. I coulda' knocked you for every last one of them bottom draw ass bitches you brought down here with you."

"Look man, you know the game…suck it up and stop acting like you was in love with the bitch. You still got one hoe left from what I hear. Get pimping, baby. I gotta go man, take it easy."

When Red hung up, Smoove was furious.

"Baby, fuck that young nigga, he still ain't got shit on you," Passion said.

"Shut up, bitch…and stay the fuck up out my conversations. I don't need no consoling hoe."

MOTIVATION: MASTERING THE GAME

He sat back on the couch and vowed that he would make both of those young niggas pay, right along with their bitches.

* * * * *

"You bullshitting, mane. I know that nigga ain't call you with that shit."

"You dig! And he was sick too, homie. I'll tell you one thing, if he could've got his hands on me, I'm sure I'd be in bad shape right now," Red said laughing. "But on a serious note though Key, you be careful with that nigga out of jail cause I think he'd try some shit, baby."

"I ain't worried about that dude. Aye, you should've told the nigga that you'd send the bitch back after you was done working the hoe, hahaha." They were laughing.

"Right, if he call me back, I'll make sure I remember that one. Dig though, I'ma catch you later, Key; be easy, baby."

* * * * *

The ground was still moist from the rain a few hours earlier, which came down in sprinkles periodically throughout the day. It was almost 2:00 a.m. and Quesha was ready to go in. Today had been a slow one for everybody, but Key demanded that they stayed on the clock. Nobody was ever allowed to return to the room before 3:00 a.m. on weekdays, and today was a Tuesday.

She was a few blocks east of Canal when he noticed her. As he continued to stalk her from an alley just up the

97

street that she was strolling, he prayed that she didn't cross over. When he knew for sure that she would be passing, he slid up against the wall of the building, careful not to alarm her as she approached.

He could hear her footsteps growing louder now. And as he saw trace of her shadow appearing, he prepared himself for the grab. Just as she stepped past the wall, he lunged at her, placing his hands around Quesha's mouth while pulling her toward the alley at the same time. It was completely dark now. He managed to drag her thirty feet as she fought for her life. She was trying her best to get a look at her abductor. Until finally he stopped, turned her around, and jammed the knife into her throat repeatedly.

"Bitch, you should've stayed in Milwaukee. This shit is real out here, don't no nigga disrespect Smoove."

She stared at him in shock, not able to scream for help. He kept his hand over her mouth the entire time until her body went limp and she stopped breathing. Then he picked her up and tossed her lifeless body into the huge dumpster. Wishing, all the while that she'd been one of those two punks who had humiliated him and stole his bread and butter.

* * * * *

By 6:00 a.m. they all knew that there had to be something wrong. They'd been calling Quesha's phone for the past three hours and she hadn't answered. The last one to see her was Venus. Her and Quesha had crossed paths inside a bar on Bourbon Street around 1:30, she told Key.

He knew Quesha had a few issues she was working

out in regards to her wife-in-laws, but she hadn't recently shown any signs of leaving the family, so he was a bit confused. The thought of her being savagely murder never crossed his mind. Things had been going well. He had a thought to go out and search for her, but decided not to. To him, the only logical idea was that she had finally fled. He just figured that it was something he hadn't anticipated.

The girls had a different feeling, they knew something was wrong. They were women, and knew how Quesha really felt about Key. He may not have been able to completely see it, but they did. The last thing she would have done was left this nigga. They wanted to go and look for her; in fact, they had an obligation to do so. But listening to his orders, they couldn't. Key told them that if she hadn't surfaced by later on that day, he would make an effort to find out more.

"If something has happened to her ain't shit we can do, this is a big ass city and we barely know our way around. It would be pointless," he said.

As he laid in the bed, he couldn't help but to think of what that nigga Smoove had said to him about getting some life insurance on yo' hoes. And for a second, he remembered the nasty call that Red had gotten from the nigga.

What if he kidnapped my bitch? What if she chose the nigga? What if he did something to her? The last thought seemed ridiculous, maybe the first two, but killing her... no way. Smoove wasn't that mad to have killed the girl. This was pimping; knocking pimps for their hoes was a part of the game. Surely Smoove respected that. *But why would she leave all her things.* She had articles there and a

99

room full of shit back in Milwaukee. This made no sense; he glanced at one of her bags on the floor and knew that she was in trouble.

Chapter 11

Key was awakened by the door slamming behind Venus as she came back into the room. He had barely gotten any sleep thinking about Quesha, but it was a new day and he had shit to do. It was money to be made, and he had two hoes to pimp.

When he came out of the shower, Venus and Classy were scanning the TV looking at news stations.

This shit is crazy, ain't nothing happened to this bitch, she done ran off. These hoes tripping, he was thinking as he wiped his hair with a towel.

"Y'all start getting ready, I'm hungry. I wanna grab something to eat," he said sitting on the bed.

* * * * *

They left the restaurant and were headed to the mall near the West Bank to do some shopping.

Key was talking to Brandon. He told him what had happened at the preliminary hearing. The judge bounded the case over for trial and his lawyer had put in a Motion for Discovery. Brandon was telling him about his next court date when Key's other line clicked.

"Hold on, B," he said after looking at his phone. It was a 504 area code, which was a New Orleans number. He thought to himself, *This must be Quesha.*

"Yeah," he said.

"Is this Keyshawn?" a male voice said sternly.

"Who is this?" Key said startled.

"This is Detective Vince Patrick with the New Orleans Police Department. Do you know a LaQuesha Madison, sir?"

"Why, what's up man?" Key said. His mind was racing; his first thought was that she'd been in jail. And even if she was, how'd this cop get his number.

"Well, sir, if you do, we need to ask you some questions."

"Questions, what questions?"

"What is your relationship to Miss Madison if you don't mind me asking?"

"Why is that important?"

"Well, we need to speak with an immediate family member. And since we noticed that you were the last person she talked to last night we thought you might be of some help," the detective had chosen his words carefully and Key knew why.

"She don't have no family. I'm her family."

"Well, sir, I'm sorry to inform you that she was murdered sometime this morning. Her body was found in a dumpster around 9:00 a.m.," he said sadly.

Key couldn't believe what he was hearing. As he pulled over to the curb and put his head on the steering wheel the girls were both looking at him with tears in their eyes.

"What happened to her?" Venus said in a trembling voice.

"Sir, are you still there? I'm sorry, but we're gonna need you to come and identify the body," he said as if it was business as usual.

"Okay, where do I come to?"

"You can call me as soon as you get in town and I'll give you directions on where to meet me." "I'm already in town," he said angrily.

This is odd, the detective was thinking. But he'd save his questions for when they met.

"Well, can you meet me at the morgue in a half an hour? Do you know how to get there?"

"I'll find it," was all Key said before he hung up.

* * * * *

Detective Patrick was looking at him as a possible suspect now. Who was he "really" to her? Possibly her pimp? They'd already determined that she must have been a prostitute. She had a purse full of condoms and cash stuffed in her bra, which was common amongst most street walkers they picked up.

And the fact that she still had money indicated to him that she wasn't the victim of a robbery. He definitely wanted to talk with this Keyshawn character, he thought looking at the phone.

Key sat there staring out of the window. *This can't be happening, dead...no, she can't be dead,* he was thinking.

Venus was sobbing now and Classy sat in the backseat letting out silent tears as she tried to understand why someone would have done this to Quesha.

"She's dead, I knew it, I told you," Venus said, rocking back and forth in the seat. Not saying a word he looked at her with watered eyes and shook his head confirming what she said.

And at that moment, Classy's weeping had gained volume as she reached over the seat embracing Venus. They knew how dangerous those streets were at night, they walked them daily. And to think that one of their own had succumbed to them was more than the two of them could bear. It didn't matter who or why, she was dead and both of them knew that it could have easily been them.

Key sat in silence thinking of what could have happened. He dialed 411 to get the directions to the morgue before pulling off.

* * * * *

He finally arrived there after nearly an hour of wrong turns and back tracking. Detective Patrick was there to meet him at the door.

"Hi, Detective Vince Patrick," he said, looking over Key's shoulder and noticing the girls in the black Escalade. Key shook his hand. "What's up?"

He had never identified a body and wasn't in the mood for pleasantries.

The detective took notice to this as well. "I'm sorry, sir; we have to go this way, the medical examiner is waiting downstairs," he said, pointing to a flight of stairs. As they walked, he asked Key question after question. Most of which he'd been truthful in answering; he had no reason to lie.

"So, you're her boyfriend you say?" the detective said studying him closely.

"Yeah."

"Do you mind me asking why you guys were in town?"

"We came for the Mardi Gras."

Of course, the detective knew that it was common for pimps to accompany their prostitutes to these events. He'd seen many similar cases over the years.

"So you guys decided to stay a few extra weeks almost, huh?"

"Yeah."

"May I ask why?"

"We just enjoyed the city," Key said, growing tired of this dude's questions.

"That must be expensive for two young people; even I couldn't afford to stay in these hotels that long. What are you guys rich?" he said, fishing for more info.

"Yeah, my mother owns a few businesses in Milwaukee, I've been spoiled my whole life," Key said as they reached the morgue entrance.

Horseshit, this fuckers obviously lying, the detective was thinking as they walked through the open door.

"Hi, Vladimir Karbachov," a tall, thin man with red hair said in a thick Russian accent.

"This is Miss Madison's boyfriend; he says she has no other family so I brought him here for the identification."

Karbachov started to say something to Key, but changed his mind once he looked at his face. He walked over to the silver drawer exposing Quesha's lifeless body from head to waist.

When Key saw her lying on the slab, he nearly threw up looking at the multiple holes that were in her upper neck and chest. He thought of how scared she must have been during all of this and couldn't fight back the tears. As he was wiping his face he said, "Yeah, that's her."

He wanted to kill whoever did this, but how. Here he was in a foreign city with no assistance.

The detective was watching his reaction to seeing the body, looking for any hint of theater performance, but he seemed genuinely devastated.

As the coroner closed the drawer he said, "It's my understanding that she's not from New Orleans so I'm going to need some information as to the shipping of her body once we finalize the autopsy results."

Key shook his head, *yes*, as he followed the doctor over to a desk.

He wrote his name and number down. "Just call me when you're done down here," he said before walking out of the door.

The detective said goodbye to the coroner and walked fast enough to catch up with him.

They were at the stairs now. "Do you mind if I ask you a few more questions?"

Key looked at him and wondered if he should. "Look man, I didn't do that shit if that's what you're thinking. If you wanna ask me something…go ahead," he said angrily.

"Where were you between the hours of 3:00 and 6:00 a.m.?"

"Sleep," he said walking.

"Can you please tell me what your girlfriend might have been doing out at that time of night alone?" he said, wanting Key to lie so he could take him in.

"I don't know probably working. Ain't that what you wanted me to say?" he said as they reached the top of the stairs. "If you have any more questions for me detective you got my number."

As he turned to walk away the detective said, "Don't you even want to know how she was killed?" Key turned around and their eyes locked.

"Those holes you saw in her neck were put there by what we think was an ice pick of some sort. It should have been you. I can't stand a coward who sits on his ass manipulating women to earn a living. And just so you know, my boys got a real good look at your other two whores out there in that pretty truck you're driving. If we see them anywhere other than the highway heading north, I'll personally see to it that your black ass becomes somebody's bitch in Angola."

His white face was now red. Key didn't say a thing as he walked out the door.

When he got in the truck the mood was somber. The girls were talking about Quesha.

"I wish I would've been with her," Venus said looking at a picture that she and Quesha took together during Mardi Gras. She had tears running down her face. Leaning back in the seat, she held the picture to her heart.

"Damn, girl!" she said out loud beginning to weep again.

"What they say happened to her?" Classy asked Key.

"They said she was stabbed with an ice pick or some shit, baby; her neck had all kinds of holes and shit in it," he said, nearly tearing up again, but he was determined to remain strong in their presence.

"Who would do some bullshit like this?" Venus said.

"That nigga, Smoove. I can see him doing something like this, you don't know him. I'm telling you he's an evil muthafucka," Classy said, looking at Key.

He didn't say a word, it was possible, but how could he prove it. Besides, Key had no time to sit around trying to figure that out; the only thing that was going through his head now was that detective's last words.

When they made it back to the room, he instructed them to pack quickly so that they could head home. He knew they had to get the fuck outta town; there was no telling what that cop had in mind.

"So we just gone leave her down here?" Venus said, feeling the need to stand up for Quesha.

"Nawh, we ain't leaving her. Look, bitch…just get packed so we can bounce," he didn't tell them what the police said to him, there was no need.

He helped them gather Quesha's things and put them in her bags. As they were doing this, the news came on with a breaking report on the story. They didn't say her name or show her picture. They just said, *A woman from Milwaukee, who police believes was a prostitute, has been murdered and stuffed in a dumpster near the French Quarters.*

They watched the TV looking for anything new, but there wasn't anything. Once they were done packing, they loaded up the truck and Key didn't waste any time getting on Interstate 10 East.

* * * * *

They were in Mississippi in less than an hour. Key wanted to see his grandmother. He called to let her know he was on his way. She was surprised to hear that her grandson was in Mississippi, but she missed him and was glad that he was coming.

He thought about what the news had said. *The police reported that she had a large amount of cash on her person so it didn't appear to be a robbery.*

The girls were both asleep when he reached back and tapped Classy on the leg.

She woke up wiping saliva from the corner of her mouth, "What's up, baby? You need some company?" she said stretching.

"Why did you say earlier that you could've seen that nigga Smoove doing that shit?"

She was thinking now, "He's a vicious nigga, baby; you should see the type of shit he does to hoes for little shit. This other girl told me that when she first got with him, they went to New York and one of the girls was trying to leave him. She said he talked her into staying and took her out by himself one night. The next morning they were all wondering where she was. One of them asked him and he slapped her saying, 'The bitch is where disloyal hoes belong.' Later on that night, the police found her body stabbed up in an abandon car." She took a breather for a minute. "That nigga's crazy like that, it's how he keeps his hoes in check. And he knew that Quesha was with you. He probably caught her and figured he'd take it out on you that way. Smoove can't stand to lose his hoes, especially to another pimp. He said all the time that if a bitch left him, she'd be going to the graveyard or the crazy house and he means that shit. I'm sure he wishes that that was you, and not her, dead down there."

Key was listening, but his thoughts were drifting off. He knew that Classy was right, that nigga was fully capable of doing that.

When she went back to sleep he called Red and told him what happen. He said the same thing Classy had told Key. Smoove was very vindictive, there were a few hoes that came up missing and later found dead with his name coming up in the mix somewhere.

"Yeah, mellow, after the way that dude was talking on the horn, it wouldn't surprise me if we found out it was him. You alright though, pimpin'?"

"Yeah, I'm good, man. I just hate that had to happen to that girl; you know."

"Yeah, I know, but this shit out here ain't peaches and cream, man. Quesha was good people; if you find out that nigga had something to do with that you can't let that shit slide."

They talked for about five more minutes before Key told Red that he was gonna call him back.

He thought about what Red said about seeking revenge, but couldn't understand it. What part of the game was this? It had nothing to do with what the pimping that he knew represented. And he was right; but what he didn't know yet was that there were niggas who took pimping to a whole other level. Anything was bound to happen when you knocked a nigga like Smoove for a bitch. Smoove was more gorilla than finesse, and this approach to the game suited him just fine.

Pimpin' wasn't an easy ride as it seemed. Key had just gotten his first bitter dose of what came with the game— *losses*! Some were simply material and could be attained again in time, but unfortunately, his was someone whom he cared about and she wouldn't be coming back. Indeed, today's lesson would be one he'd never forget.

Chapter 12

Pearl-Jean Watson lived a simple life in the small town of McComb, Mississippi. She preferred tending to her garden of roses and reading books by Maya Angelou over anything else in the world. The only other exception was reading the Word. She attended service four days out of the week and was considered to be one of the most active members in the congregation. At sixty-seven, she was in good shape; she walked daily and did light exercise training a few days out of the week. Her figure was as slim as it had been when she was in her twenties and had it not been for the salt and pepper hair she could have easily been mistaken for being in her forties. Pearl had aged gracefully indeed.

She was on the front porch sitting in her favorite chair when Keyshawn arrived. When he parked the truck, she wasn't sure it was him until he emerged wearing that huge smile he'd had since he was a baby.

"Hey, grandma," he said as she came down the stairs to give him a hug.

"Hey, baby," she said, kissing him on the cheek. "They must not be feeding you right up there, you done lost some weight," she said looking at his stomach.

"I know," he was smiling. "I miss yo' food, mama don't cook like she used to no more."

The girls were looking out the windows. "Who you bring with you, why they just sitting in there looking?" she said, waving at them.

Key motioned for them to get out. "Keyshawn, whose truck is that?"

"It's mine grandma," he said, hoping she wasn't going to pry any further. She chose to save that for later.

The girls walked up. "How you young ladies doing?"

"How you doing, ma'am?" they both said almost in unison.

"Grandma, this is Venus and Crystal," he said, looking at Classy with a smile.

"Oh, both of you are some beautiful young women," she said overlooking their clothing. They hadn't toned it down, and Key cursed himself for his lack of thoroughness. "Y'all come on inside."

Some of the neighbors were starting to get nosy, and she thought it may have been because of the girls' attire. Either that, or the big black truck that was parked on the block.

When they were all inside, she offered everyone something to drink and came back with three glasses of coke.

"So how long y'all gonna be staying?" she said to Key.

"We can't stay long grandma; I have to be back in Milwaukee tomorrow."

"Where y'all coming from?" she looked puzzled.

"New Orleans."

Key knew that what she really wanted to say was, *What are you doing down here with these two girls?*

They talked for an hour before his aunt Tina came through the door.

"Mama, whose truck...Hey, nephew."

"Hey, aunt Tina," he said hugging her.

"What you doing down here?" she was eyeing the girls.

"I was just stopping by to see y'all, where Mal at?"

"Mama didn't tell you he went to the Army?"

"Nawh," he said looking at Pearl."

"Child, it slipped my mind, you can't expect me to remember everything at my age."

Key wasn't surprised, Mal was the Army type. "I see you brought some friends."

He introduced them again.

"Girl, what you wearing? Keyshawn, this girl needs to put some clothes on," Tina said referring to Classy. "I know they ain't dressing that way in Milwaukee this time of year it's too cold," she said laughing.

Classy was flushing.

"Tina, don't you gotta be at work soon?" Pearl said looking at the clock.

"Yes, I just came to get my phone, mama." She went upstairs.

* * * * *

A few hours later, Pearl was in the kitchen finishing dinner. They all ate and Key went back in the kitchen to help her clean up.

They were alone and she figured now was a good time to see what her grandson had been up to. She was wiping a plate dry. "That's a nice truck you got yourself out there Keyshawn. Your mama told me you helped her buy another house too."

"Yeah, you should've seen where they were living at grandma. I had to help her."

"Keyshawn, your mother can take care of herself. She may not tell you this, but she's worried to death about you boy. Now, I don't know what you doing, but I can tell you that fast money don't last baby. You can make a million dollars out there in them streets, but it's gone cost you three million more to keep it."

He didn't say a thing; he kept washing dishes as she gave him almost the same lecture that she did the night before he left.

"And I know you don't have those girls out there selling their bodies?" Pearl stopped what she was doing and looked at him waiting for a response. "Nawh, grandma, they just my friends." She knew he was lying.

"I sure hope not, cause we raised you better than that."

"Hey, grandma, can you make me that German chocolate cake again?" he said, desperate to change the subject.

"It's gone take too long, Keyshawn. I don't feel like doing all that now," Pearl said, leaning on the table, knowing that she wasn't about to get out of this one. "Come on, grandma."

"Boy, go get me the mix out of that cabinet and gone sit down in the living room. I knew your butt was gonna come down here wanting me to bake something."

"I'll help you."

"Nawh, gone in there, you just gonna be in my way, yo' lil girl friends probably miss you anyway," she laughed. Pearl could never say no to any of her grandchildren, she spoiled them all. But it didn't matter because they were her joy. And even though Keyshawn got on her nerves sometimes, he was still her favorite.

After they had cake, the girls were tired. Pearl showed them to a room and when they hit the mattress they were out almost instantly.

"Those girls are too young to be that tired. When y'all get back to Milwaukee you make sure they get some rest." Key didn't say anything.

"You hear me, Keyshawn?" she was dead serious now.

"Yeah, grandma, I hear you," was all he could say.

They sat up and talked until 2:00 a.m. Pearl had read scriptures from the Bible for him, told him more stories about his mother growing up, and they played gin rummy.

When Tina arrived home from work she said, "I knew y'all was still gonna be up, two night owls. Well, I'm going to bed I'll see y'all tomorrow."

"I better go to bed myself; this boy done came down here and threw my whole schedule off."

But Pearl really didn't mind, she enjoyed the quality time.

* * * * *

When Key woke up, the girls were in the living room talking to Pearl.

"Mama's downstairs trying to convert them girls, you better go get 'em before she have them at Bible study with her tonight," Tina said laughing. She'd always been known for her bluntness and humor.

When he went downstairs, the girls were so tuned in to Pearl's words that they hardly even saw him enter the room. When he came out of the kitchen, they were still locked in. He knew he had to get them out of her hands before Tina was right.

As Key took a shower he thought about Quesha. He had to make an effort to try and find her family. He'd never met a single one of them. The only person he knew of her being connected to was the girl she used to live with, Tamala. He made a mental note to go by there when he got back in town. He'd chosen not to tell Pearl about Quesha, and hoped Venus and Classy hadn't mentioned a word of it, otherwise she was about to let him have it.

After the shower, he grabbed the breakfast that Pearl left him on the stove before he joined them. Once he ate they talked for a little while longer before he announced that they had to be going. They were all headed back to the truck now.

"Y'all take care of yourselves," Pearl said as the girls were getting in the truck waving goodbye.

"Keyshawn you remember what I said, and you make sure that you call that girl's family and let them know what happen to her."

He was stuck when she said that.

"They told me all about it, I don't want you to say nothing, just make sure you call that girl's family."

His head was down and when he looked up she just shook her head and gave him a hug.

"You call and let me know when you make it back too, okay."

"Alright, love you grandma."

"Love you too, baby."

When he got in the truck he turned over the engine.

"Who told her about yesterday?" they were both quiet until Venus spoke up.

"We were talking and she kept asking me what was wrong. Your grandmother got a way of pulling shit out of people."

Key wasn't tripping; he just wanted to know who cracked.

"Yeah, I know," was all he said. She had the same effect on most people.

Chapter 13

After making it back the first thing he did was went to Tamala's. She broke down when he told her about Quesha, and then she became irate and disrespectful toward him as if he'd done it.

Once he was able to calm her down he got some information on Quesha's mother. When he went by the house a woman answered the door, recognizing the resemblance, he figured this must have been her mother, which she was.

He told her about Quesha's death and to his astonishment she didn't seem affected by it as a mother should have been. She dropped a few tears, and then asked him, "Did she leave anything behind?"

"Anything like what?" he said confused.

"You know, like some money or something?"

"What?" he couldn't believe what he was hearing.

"I heard she was doing good for herself," she was looking straight at the floor fiddling with her hands. Her fingers were all burned at the tips and suddenly it dawned on him, this lady was a crackhead. When he first came into the house he looked around and figured she might have just ran into some bad luck. But as Key studied her more carefully it became clear to him.

"Well, you don't have to worry about the funeral arrangements, I'm taking care of that, just let the rest of the family know."

"Okay, you think that you could borrow me a few dollars, I got a son back there and he ain't ate nothing all day," she said wiping her nose.

He got up from the couch thinking, *this bitch*, then reached in his pocket and gave her a hundred-dollar bill. Her face lit up like a bright summer day. As Key was leaving, he gave her his number and told her to call him in a few days with the number of people who might be attending the funeral service.

When he got in the truck he knew why Quesha never spoke of her mother. He doubted if she'd tell anyone about the funeral, but he'd done his part.

* * * * *

The next day, they called to inform him that her body was ready to be shipped. He made arrangements and began preparing for Quesha's burial. After going to her mom's house three days in a row without getting an answer he finally gave up. Not knowing what to put on the obituary, he had Tamala prepare it and they used a picture that she took a couple of days prior to her demise.

* * * * *

The funeral was held a week after Quesha's body was flown back to Milwaukee. None of her family showed up, not even the mother. In fact, the only people who attended were some of her friends and a few hoes that had known Quesha from her short career in the life.

After everything was over, Key was relieved; the whole experience was overwhelming but he had to make sure she'd been given a proper burial. At the service, he got a sense of what her life must have been like being surrounded by outsiders continuously. He knew that if none of her family were there now that they probably never had been.

* * * * *

Key and T. A. had some issues with the plug and it looked as though things were about to change.

"I been calling them folks for three weeks now Key, and both the numbers I had are disconnected now."

"What you think is going on, T?"

"I don't know, but this ain't never happened, anytime I call Oscar he always answered. And one of the numbers I had was his home phone. The shit's got me paranoid. I turned off that line I used when I called him. It gotta be something going on. I still have two hundred grand that the dude ain't called about or nothing. What nigga you know ain't coming to get that kind of money?"

"Yeah, something's definitely not right, what you gone do with the cash?"

"What can I do, shit, but if the cat don't come get it soon, he can chalk it up, baby."

"Well, I guess that's the end of the connect, huh?"

"Not necessarily, we could get with them other people, but the numbers ain't nowhere near as sweet as Oscar's. Plus, I ain't fucked with them in a minute. Personally, I think we should back up for a while. If you want to do something I can introduce y'all, but that shit'll be at your own risk."

Key began to ponder it all. Brandon was moving most of the shit but he was leery about fucking around right now because of the open case. This meant that if Key grabbed anything, he'd be doing a lot more leg work on his own. Something that he didn't want to do, and then there was the issue with this new plug. After weighing out his options he decided to keep his distance from the weed right now, too many risks.

"You know what, T? I think I'll pass on them maybe your boy will surface."

"Yeah, and if he do, I'm not too sure I wanna fuck with him either. I think I'm gonna stick to selling pussy man, and that may not be such a bad idea for you either." Key nodded in concurrence.

"You did good out there didn't you?" it was more of a comment than a question. "You know as soon as that shit happened to yo' people it was all over the wire with that nigga Smoove's name all on it. That's the game though, Key. A nigga just gotta keep on pimping. You gonna have many cats like that buster to deal with in the future. Let them keep doing that sucka shit while you peeling 'em for their hoes."

* * * * *

The F.B.I.'s main field office for Milwaukee was located in the central business district downtown on Water and Mason Street. Housed in the twelve-story Franklin D. Roosevelt building, the agency occupied the top three floors. The Special Agent In Charge (SAIC) was Sidney Bender. His office was on the twelfth floor overlooking the Milwaukee River.

He was in the middle of an important meeting over the phone with Washington when his secretary buzzed him on another line.

"Can you hold for one second please? Yes, Agent Bender."

"Mr. Bender, Agent Greg Daley is here for his one o'clock meeting."

"Thank you, Morgan…you can send him in."

When Greg Daley entered the room, Agent Bender was still on the phone; he held up a finger and pointed toward a chair in front of his desk. Sidney Bender was a big man at six feet, four inches tall. A straight, to the point kind of guy who had little time for small talk. He talked on the phone for another two minutes before hanging up.

"Here's the deal Daley, we got a call from our people down in New Orleans. Seems they had a Milwaukee girl found dead with no perp in custody. Police did their little investigation and it led them to a young man here who's believed to be the girls pimp."

Interrupting, Daley said, "So she was a prostitute? How old?"

Shuffling through some papers Bender finally said, "Yeah, and she was twenty from what our records indicate. Don't worry I'll have Morgan make copies of all this stuff and get them to your desk before two o'clock. Anyway, the detectives on the case interviewed the pimp and he doesn't believe that he had anything to do with it. He told the detective that he was at the hotel sleeping at the time of the murder and his story checked out, a clerk furnished them with tapes and his vehicle hadn't moved between those hours. Another clerk told him that he came back to the hotel with two of his other prostitutes and didn't leave out for the rest of his shift."

Interrupting again Daley said curiously, "So it's my guess that we're going after this guy for *interstate trafficking* right?"

"Yes, of course; but somebody has to know why this girl was killed and possibly by whom. The police have ruled out robbery because the girl still had nearly a thousand dollars in her possession when they found her body. What I need you to do is get to those other two girls that he had with them and see what they know. If it wasn't a robbery, then it's possible it was some kind of vendetta. Right after the girl was killed our man hauled ass back up here. Two officers were able to get photos of the girls outside of the morgue while he was identifying the body. We already have a file on him; he's had a few juvenile runins but nothing serious. Bottom line, Daley…is we need to get to these girls because he's not gonna talk. I've assigned Agent Chan to this case with you and our goal is to get her on the inside."

There was a knock at the door.

"Come in."

"I'm sorry I'm late, sir. I had a 12:30 with *special operations* and it ran a little late."

"Have a seat, Li Chan I'm sure you know Greg Daley, he's gonna be working with you on this one."

They both looked at one another and nodded. "I'll continue, Daley you can fill her in on what she missed later. As I was saying, we want Chan to get in on the inside so this may consume a great deal of your time. I'll have your caseload moved around to another agent and…"

"Sir, may I ask why are we about to spend so much time on this guy, there really doesn't seem to be much to pursue," Chan said looking at Bender.

"I'm with you on that, but this is coming from our regional office in Madison. I spoke with the Chief over there. It seems that she's been getting calls from our offices around the country reporting everything from grand theft's to murders involving pimps from Milwaukee. They've decided to form a special unit to investigate future cases.
But the team hasn't been put in place yet."

Another knock at the door.

Irritated he said, "Come in."

"Sir, this just came in from New Orleans," Morgan said, handing him an envelope.

"Thank you, Morgan. Oh, and can you take this and prepare files for these agents?" he said handing her the file. "Yes, sir, right away."

He opened the envelope and pulled out some photos. "Okay folks, these are our new friends. This is Keyshawn Watson, age nineteen; the cops took this picture of him leaving the morgue. And these two must be a part of his flock."

The agents were studying the pictures.

"You can keep the photos for your files, and I'm sorry this wasn't done earlier, but I just received everything right before this meeting. Get in there and find out what you can about this young girl's murder, Chan; and I'm sure that by the time we're done, we'll have this Watson character on a nice solid case of trafficking at the least. Morgan will have those files for you and I'll expect a full briefing by noon tomorrow. Any questions?"

"Yes, do we have a location as to where he may be housing these girls or where he's staying?" Daley said.

"All we have is in those file, I'm sure that's the least of our worries agent."

Greg Daley was in his second year at the bureau. He was a good agent, but at times not too keen with his questions. Something Agent Bender had gotten used to.

* * * * *

After they left the meeting they went to collect their files from Morgan, then went to work sorting out all the information they had. The plates on the black Escalade were registered to his mother Michelle Watson, but they doubted if the address was his residence. The phone number they had was the phone that N.O.P.D. provided them with and when they checked to see if it was active, they got an answer from a male who they figured had to be their target. His driver's license carried the same address as the truck. However, when they ran the truck for parking tickets with the city's municipal department two citations had been issued at a separate address, something that they made a note of. And finally after three hours of sitting, making phone calls, and searching their internal network for information they decided to take a break.

* * * * *

"Ma', I gotta go," Key said then kissed Michelle on the cheek.

"I'm gonna call you later bro," Keysha said.

"Alright, and it's about time you learned how to cook, that food wasn't bad. I'll see y'all later." Michelle and Keysha had cooked dinner for Key and Brandon.

He hopped in the SL600 Mercedes, a new toy he bought for himself. Key was on his way home to pick up the girls to go out on an outing before they went back to work. After a week and a half, it was time to get back to the regularly scheduled program.

"I see our boy's been doing a little shopping," Agent Daley said looking through a pair of binoculars.

"A little shopping...that guy's in a sixty-thousand dollar vehicle. I've got a feeling that's he's doing something other than running these girls. But we'll see huh?" Chan said, following behind him at a safe distance.

When Key made it home, he parked the Benz in the garage and went inside.

"Well, at least now we know for sure this is where he's living. And I bet those girls are right in there with him" Daley said looking at the townhouse trying to see any trace of bodies moving around.

"I think we've done enough for today. Tomorrow, I want to start some type of profile on the girls. Chan was starting to pull off.

"Hold on a second, somebody's coming out."

They all came out and piled into Key's truck that was parked on the street. As they rode past the agent's car they paid no attention to the black Monte Carlo with tented windows parked down the street from the house.

When the truck made the left turn at the corner, Chan performed a U-turn in pursuit.

"Notify M.P.D. and have them pulled over, I want those girls' names and anything else they can find out."

Daley made the call and within minutes they were stopped by police.

* * * * *

"What's the problem officer?" Key said, calming down. The cop was looking at him with his flash light.

"You just seemed to be speeding a bit, that's all. Can I have your driver's license please?"

"Here you go," Key said, knowing full well he wasn't speeding.

The officer got back in the car and got on the radio. "I have this guy pulled over, now what do you want me to do?" The dispatcher called him back with the agent's phone number, he called them.

"This is Officer Mathis with the M.P.D., I have the subject. Do you want me to hold him until you get here?"

"No officer, that won't be necessary, but what we do need is the names of the two females with him and any other information that you can pull from them please."

"Okay, I'll try; by law passengers don't have to talk with police unless there's a criminal investigation and at this point it's just a traffic stop."

"I'm well aware of that officer, hopefully their naive to the law and won't mind furnishing you with the information."

"I'll give you a call back when I'm done."

Mathis didn't like the Feds and here he was doing their dirty work for them, he felt like a puppet. But his shift had just begun and he wanted something to do otherwise it would be another long night.

Once he walked back to the Escalade he made up some bullshit excuse about checking the girl's names for warrants and they gave him their IDs. Both were out-ofstate IDs one from North Carolina and the other from Maryland. He thought this was odd as he looked over the cards on his way back to the car. He called the agents back.

"I have both their IDs here."

"Do the pictures match?" Daley said.

Offended, Mathis responded, "What you guys at the bureau think you're the only ones who knows how to check IDs too now I take it?"

Daley noticed that he'd offended the officer's intelligence.

"I'm sorry; we're just trying to be thorough, that's all, officer."

"Yeah," he said then read off the data on the cards.

They thanked him then informed Mathis that he could release them. He returned back to the truck.

"Now that didn't take too long did it, you're free to go just watch your speed sir," he said while handing everyone their IDs.

Bullshit, Key was thinking as he walked off. "Y'all see that plastic ass smile he hit us with, that punk knew I wasn't speeding he just wanted to fuck with us."

* * * * *

"You ready to turn it in, Li?"

"Yeah, I have paperwork that's due in the morning; I hate that shit. And I'm due in the court at ten."

"You think these girls will be able to give us anything about that murder?"

"I hope so," she said, viewing the information they just received.

Chapter 14

At the noon briefing they went over all the intelligence they were able to gather first.

"The first subjects name is Crystal Milton; she's twenty-two from Baltimore, Maryland. Our records show that she's had six arrests nationwide in four states. One in her home town for theft, one in Boston for prostitution; two in Miami for prostitution; and another prostitution charge in Atlanta, Georgia as well as possession of THC. All of these charges occurred within the last three years, and she's wanted in at least two of these states for bail jumping," Chan was shuffling through more papers.

"The other one is Venus Franklin, nineteen, from Charlotte, North Carolina. We don't have her on file for any arrests," Chan said overlooking her file.

They'd gathered other information about their families, schools they attended, etc., but none of this held any relevance in the meeting.

"So, did we get a location on these people's residences?" Bender said, rubbing his temples.

"Yes, we tailed Watson from his mother's house in his new Mercedes to a townhouse downtown. He went in and fifteen minutes later emerges with the two girls," Daley said, handing him the pictures.

Bender scanned them. "This kid is nineteen buying these types of vehicles, did you do a *disclosure order* with the dealer?"

"No, we didn't want to ring any alarms this early, we figured we'd do that once we came close to wrapping the case up," Chan said.

"Good thinking," he said handing her the pictures. "Okay let's go over strategies," he was leaning back in his chair as both agents began laying out the plans they developed earlier that morning.

* * * * *

Key had awakened around noon. He contemplated his next set of moves before getting out of bed that afternoon. Sure he was pleased with his accomplishments so far, but wasn't anywhere near where he'd dreamed of being. The game had a way of increasing ones appetite and he was no exception. The more you achieved, the more you craved. And his ego wouldn't allow him to be content. It was this part of him that was dying to be fed. Making the decision to concentrate solely on his pimping, he knew that if he wanted to attain all that his craft had to offer, he needed to fetch and attract every hoe that came across his path.

Venus and Classy had bookings in brothels near Reno, Nevada for eight weeks. After driving them to Mitchell International, Key stopped at a service station for gas. While paying the attendant, a voice behind him said, "That's a nice truck you're driving, mind if I ask what year it is?

When he turned around he was startled by her beauty. Standing at 5'2" with a perfect Colgate smile, she had his undivided attention. Wearing terry cloth workout pants and a jacket; you could see every curve her sculpted frame had to offer. After a complete scan from head to toe, he locked into her slanted eyes.

"It's to the year."

"I love that truck, must cost a fortune." she said appealing to his ego.

"Nawh, it ain't that much. Nothing that hard work can't afford," he said, stepping to the side so she could get to the counter.

"Hard work, you look too young to even know what that is," she said with a small chuckle. "I don't even see how you could afford to buy something like that; I wish I could stand one."

"You can baby, you just gotta find out how," he was in one hundred percent working mode now.

"I guess," she said walking to the door. When they got outside, she could feel him looking at her ass and knew that her mission was complete.

"Can I look inside?" she strolled up to the passenger door and acted amazed by the interior.

After pumping his gas, he got in. "So what's your name anyway, baby?"

She was leaning into the window. "You first."
Once he announced who he was, she responded by shaking his hand.

"So, you gonna tell me your name or what?" he said with a question mark on his face.

"Oh, I'm sorry, my name's Kimmie."

"Well, can I call you later?"

"How about I call you, I wanna know what your secret is. Since you make everything sound so easy."

After he gave her his number, they chatted briefly before saying goodbyes.
When she made it to the vehicle, she phoned Agent Daley. "I made contact."

"That was fast, you think he smelled anything fishy?"

"Not a chance, he gave me his number and I'm sure he'll be waiting for me to call. I'll meet you at the office in a half an hour."

When Key drove off he thought about what was in store for Kimmie if she called. He was sure she'd be working in no time, she was ready to start asking questions and the Escalade had her in awe.

If only he knew what door that simple conversation had just opened. But her intro and approach couldn't have been in a better setting, leaving his mind totally at ease.

* * * * *

Agent Chan let a few days pass before she made contact with Key again. At which time they both agreed to meet for lunch at a restaurant downtown.

When Key arrived, she was already inside and her partner Greg Daley was on location close by picking up the conversation from the wire that was planted in a dummy cell phone.

"The subject just parked valet, he's coming in now," Daley said, conversing with Chan on the agency cell. She said okay, turned off the phone, and placed it in her purse.

Key was lead to the table by a Latin waiter who disappeared and quickly returned with a pitcher of water.

"Was that you in that red car, Key?" Chan said, unable to avoid looking at the diamond-encrusted cursive Q connected to the chain draping from his neck. A remembrance of Quesha Madison she thought.

"That depends on who's asking?" he said sitting down. She almost got nervous for a second before realizing it was a joke.

"The F.B.I." she said, playing along.

He looked at her and started laughing. "Real funny." She gave him a humorous smile.

Meanwhile, Daley was sweating bullets. "She's nuts," he said out loud to himself.

"I like that piece, but why the Q? And please don't tell me you gave me a fake name."

"No, it's for someone that I lost that's all."

"Oh, how sweet," Daley said listening. "Sorry to hear that, must have been a close friend?"

"Yeah, one of my girlfriends, she was killed."

"What! That's terrible, how did something like that happen?" she asked, careful not to sound too anxious for the answer.

"I don't know, they found her dead in a dumpster," he was looking at the menu remembering her face in the morgue on the iron slab.

Chan braced herself as she made the next statement. "Oh, my God! I hope they found the person who did that, please tell me they did?"

Daley couldn't believe she made it this far so fast. And he was praying for any clue that they might be able to use in their investigation.

Chan was near perspiration as she wanted on his response. Looking up from the menu, he stared at her for a moment before speaking.

"Can we talk about something else, that's really not one of my favorite things to discuss."

With her heart rate slowing down she said, "Sure, I understand, I'm sorry."

"That's okay, so what you ordering?"

Daley was disappointed, but this was only the beginning. And they hadn't expected to get anything out of him anyway.

They talked and asked general questions about each other while waiting for the food. Chan was answering each one thoughtfully so that she'd remember what she'd said, if need be in the future. A technique she'd learned at the bureau's training facility in Langley, Virginia.

"So, when are you going to tell me your secret? Let's not forget I came to take lessons," she said with a smile.

"I'm a pimp," he said, as bluntly as he could, waiting to see her reaction.

"Oh, I see, so you want to teach me how to pimp?

He laughed. "And I see you being funny again, huh, Kimmie. No, but I wanna show you how to have whatever you want, when you want it, baby. You just can't be scared to go get it, and sometimes take it if necessary," Key was in rare form and had she not been here doing a job his presentation may have reached her. Chan could definitely see how he was able to spark interest in a young girl in search of a future.

"I like the sound of that; I'm just not sure I'm up ready for the task."

"You will be after the proper training, trust me. If I had a dollar for every time I heard that, baby…I'd be a millionaire," Key said lying, but it was a part of his job.

"So, when do we start this training?"

"We started the other day, you just didn't know it."

Chan smiled. She was used to hearing conversation from her colleagues at the bureau it had been three years since her last real relationship, which ended sourly after the guy left her for a girl with wealthy parents. That's when she joined the F.B.I. After she turned twenty-one, putting her energy toward work, hoping it would erase or ease some of the pain she was silently going through. With the exception of a few office flings, Chan kept her distance from men. But at times, she yearned for companionship, and lunch with this man wasn't making it any better.

Chapter 15

Over the next month, Chan was able to work her way into Key's operation without blowing her cover. She claimed to have a few rich men who wanted to do things for her but she never pursued their offers. Hearing this, Key coached her on how to get things out of these men and she would come back to him with cash. On a few occasions, she even asked him to take her to Western Union (The wires and all the monies she brought to him came out of the Operations Expense Fund of the bureau. The government had millions of dollars set aside from mostly drug money they sized during busts of dealers throughout the country and abroad. The cash is allotted to the main four law enforcement agencies; F.B.I., D.E.A., A.T.F., and U.S. Customs. They used this cash to fund more operations in their fight against crime).

Her boss, SAIC Bender wanted to bug her house, but after much thought decided that the risk was too great. Electing to go with a wiretap instead, which a judge granted after hearing several hours of conversations with Chan and Key.

Greg Daley kept constant track of Venus and Classy's movements in Nevada through agents in Reno who paid visits to the brothels they worked at once a week. There had been strict orders from Bender to never attempt to make contact or question them in any way. It was his position that Chan had the best chance at obtaining the information they were looking for.

The two agents were building a firm case on Key already. The wiretaps proved to be their strongest weapon. In a little over a month and a half, they had a list of charges. Among them were, Interstate Transportation of a person engaging in Prostitution, three counts of party to the crime of Identity Theft, money laundering, credit card fraud; aiding and abetting. An indictment of these three charges alone would ensure him a sentence of at least twenty-five to thirty years on a plea.

Through Agent Chan's mingling with Key, they were also able to start files on T.A. and Red as well. Investigations into Red's Chicago activities and T.A. internet operations had begun immediately by special agents in Milwaukee and Chicago.

Bender was pleased with the investigations success so far. He coined the name *Operation Three Amigo's*, and planned to make arrests simultaneously on all subjects involved once the details were thoroughly covered and the U.S.

Attorney's Office were able to secure indictments from a grand jury.

* * * * *

Key was at his flat addressing two new recruits he'd recently bumped. The first one was Paris, a name he had given her himself because she was a splitting image of the hotel heiress. She was white with brunette hair, that he had dyed blond, slim and stood six feet three inches tall in heels.

Standing next to her was Chrissy, she was a plain Jane natural blond who didn't have a clue as to a real whore's duties when he met her. Her frame was petite and flawless, and she had the face of a Playboy Bunny. The only issue was her nose being much too long and her teeth were jacked up. But after sending her to a plastic surgeon and a series of dental procedures Hugh Hefner would have traded his magazine empire for this one.

Key finessed them out of the hands of some clown who was sleep to what he had. They were working a track on the south side of Milwaukee that was prime turf for junkies.

"The last thing I'm gonna have in this family is a bitch who doesn't wanna be a team player," he said sitting back on the huge leather sectional.

"But, daddy, I was trying to make sure I wasn't late for my date. I thought your money was more important than me helping this bitch pack some clothes," Paris said, rolling her eyes at Chrissy.

They had gotten into a small cat fight and spilled a beverage all over the living room carpet.

"Shut up, bitch, did I tell you to say anything. As a result of that little stupid ass brawl you still missed your appointment and I'm late taking this hoe to the airport, not to mention the fact that you just assisted in fuckin' up the carpet. Listen, both of you hoes get outta my sight, and call them tricks up to tell 'em there's gonna be a small delay."

Just then, the postal worker was at the door with a package. It was priority mail from Venus and Classy. Key had instructed them to send all his money this way in money orders to avoid paying high fees at Western Union.

When he opened the envelope the seventeen thousand they said would be there was intact, all in money orders and travelers checks.

He almost forgot about the current issue at hand until Paris came back into the living room.

"See, this is what you suppose to be doing right now bitch, getting me some fucking money," he said waving the trap at her.

"I'm sorry, baby, you know I'll make it up." And she would, it wasn't unusual for Paris to drop three or four thousand dollars in one night on Key sometimes. He knew Milwaukee was good ground for a white girl to work, so Paris and Chrissy along with Kimmie worked an escort service that he'd formed.

Chrissy did ok, but he knew that she could do a lot better. So Key critiqued and educated her daily in an effort to bring her up to speed with the others.

Kimmie stayed consistent with his cash as well. She had specific clients requesting her, but the callers were various agents phoning in from the bureau. And at times when she was forced to go on random calls, she'd simply go and tell the client who she was, show him her badge, and still take his money. After some serious threats of jail they'd go away never to tell a soul out of fear of what might happen. But this rarely happened most of the time she'd have fake dates arranged for days at a time to limit her exposure. At the moment, she was suppose to be in Lake Geneva servicing a client, but was actually at the field office assisting with the investigations on T.A. and Red. Chan's mission was to lie around and wait for Venus and Classy to return, which was a few weeks away now.

Paris came over to the couch and sat next to Key. "Daddy, how long you gone make me wait?" she said looking at him seductively. She was a nympho and if she could fuck all day she probably would.

"Did you and that bitch kiss and make up?" he said, ignoring her question.

"Yeah, we cool baby," she said, pressing up against him.

"Good, don't let no shit like that happen again. And get yo' horny ass off me bitch you got work to do."

Key hadn't touched her sexually since he had her. She thought he wasn't attracted to her because the last dude she was with kept his Johnson in her mouth and pussy as much as he could. So she didn't quite understand this kick Key was on, she though fucking was a thing that pimps valued before cash. When in fact it was the total opposite, but she was turned out by a sucka.

When she got up and went into the room he was somewhat relieved. The bitch almost got him; it had been months since he'd had some pussy—something that all good pimps experienced. It was the number one test and if you couldn't pass with flying colors you weren't cut out for the role. How could you effectively stand on a hoe and be weak to her womanhood at the same time, impossible! He had yet to touch anyone of his hoes, except Quesha, and this sometimes amazed Key, but more importantly, it educated him. A chick respected a nigga's mind, she could get dick anywhere. Key knew this had to be true, otherwise why were these hoes paying him so well. However, he was no fool either; he knew that eventually all these bitches would demand their fair share of cock, he just hoped he'd be a million dollars ahead of 'em by then. The thought of that made him smile, and then he wondered how long would nature allow him to keep doing this. Contrary to that slick shit many pimps kicked, he wasn't about to be somewhere pulling on his own dick and he definitely wasn't about to give himself to some square bitch who hadn't contributed to his success. This pimp shit was a game of wits and to win you had to be mentally fit.

I gotta keep beatin' these hoes at their own game, just like this white bitch she's used to niggas not being able to resist her, not me I'm...

"Daddy."

His thoughts were interrupted, and took him out of his daze.

"What?"

"My date in Chicago says he gonna ride up here to get me, what should I do?" Chrissy said dumbfounded.

"Wait for him to get here, what else you gone do."

She was about the dizziest hoe he'd had thus far. And he was growing tired of her slowness; in fact he'd grown tired of both them in general. They had been staying with him for nearly a month and he was starting to miss Classy and Venus. At least they were quiet, peaceful, and would let him think. These two were totally opposite; one was constantly trying to con sex from him while the other needed help tying her shoes. He would have to make other living arrangements for them ASAP before they drove him up the wall.

Just as Paris was leaving on her way to catch her date, she walked past him cutting her eye before slamming the door on her way out.

That bitch is crazy! What have I gotten myself into, he thought to himself. But it was the life of a pimp.

Chapter 16

Key was watching an amateur boxing match on *ESPN* when his phone rang. "Hello."

"What's happenin', lil buddy? I got some holla for you," T.A. said.

"What might that be, big homie?" Key said, turning the TV down.

"I'm looking at buying this club and I was thinking you might want in on it. I'ma buy the building myself, but I was thinking of having a couple of partner's share in the venture with me. Red on his way up here, I talked to him about it. So if you free, we can all go look at it and discuss the details if you're interested in getting on board."

"Okay, just call and let me know when you ready to check it out."

* * * * *

Key met them at the place a few hours later. It was located on the northwest side of town and was being run by a couple in their thirties. When they went inside Key didn't like the size of the place and he shared his views about that with TA.

"Well, I was thinking we could knock a few walls down and expand it. There's an apartment on the other side of this wall and two more upstairs. I want to convert the whole building, they just renewed their license with the common council, and if we do happen to have some issues with that my people have a good relationship with the alderman over here. And for a couple of stacks, we can be cleared through zoning to start remodeling the way we want it."

"So, how much of your end are you willing to share," Red said, looking around.

"I'll take fifty percent of the business and y'all can split the other fifty however way you choose. There won't be no rent with me buying the building so I think that's a good deal. I'll pay for all the remodeling too. Y'all would just invest in the business itself."

Key liked this idea. "Cool, I'm in," was all he said. Red followed and they both agreed to split the other end in half at twenty-five percent ownership each.

"How long you think its gone take for all this remodeling shit T.?" Red said.

"I'm closing on the building tomorrow and I'll have the contractors start as soon as that's done. They assured me that it shouldn't take any more than six to eight weeks. And like I said, we already have license so all we'll have to do is furnish and stock the place and we'll be ready to roll," he said, patting them both on the shoulders. "You boys can thank me for this later. I'm not gone keep pulling you young niggas coats to shit, I done told y'all," he laughed jokingly. When they made it back outside, they chatted for a few minutes.

"Say, mane...did this cat tell you about the fit his bitch threw on him last light?" T.A. said to Key referring to one of Red's hoes.

"Nawh, but I got one who can't seem to keep her hands to herself, the bitch stormed out my crib this afternoon in some serious heat."

"Haha, you must be talking about one of them snow bunnies? They can get feisty when it comes to that P., when I knock one I make sure she have her own area cause I'm not humping every time the hoe give a nigga some bread," Red said.

Down the block in an unmarked vehicle, Agent Daley watched them. He documented the location on a digital recorder and headed back to the field office. There was no need for him to stick around, he listened to the phone conversation T.A. and Key had earlier so he knew why they were meeting there.

* * * * *

Key continued to hold his ground with Paris. And when Classy and Venus were due back in Milwaukee he was relieved, he'd have some more people in the house to act as a cushion between him and her horny ass.

When Agent Chan caught wind that they were returning, she was prepared to start her next phase of the investigation. She used an apartment that was set-up for her by the bureau, but under Bender's she would sleep in the house with Venus and Classy whenever they were there, becoming their best friend.

As Key was leaving to pick them up from the airport Chan and the other girls were cleaning the upstairs.

"Kimmie," Key said from the stairs.

"Yes, daddy?"

"Get dressed. I want you to ride with me to pick these bitches up."

Paris was listening and wanted to join them.

"Daddy, I wanna go," she said as Chan was walking down the stairs.

"Did anybody call yo' name girl? We'll be back in a minute," Chan said jokingly.

"Shut up, bitch. I wasn't talking to you," she snapped back.

"I'll be back in a minute, get that cleaning done. We all gonna do something a lil later today, okay," Key said. She didn't answer. "You hear what I said, bitch?"

"Yeah, okay," she shouted from the upstairs bedroom before turning the vacuum cleaner back on. She was pissed and jealous; Paris always wanted time with Key alone. And she hated the fact that he was taking Kimmie and not her. She hardly ever got a chance to spend time with him and it was beginning to get on her nerves. Paris was extremely needy and had been this way for most of her life. Growing up with no father, Paris was constantly searching for attention and approval from a man.

When she was a young teenager, she overheard her mother telling a friend how weak she thought her daughter was, and then she went on for another ten minutes about how life may have been different if she'd had a boy instead of a girl. After hearing this coming from her own mother, her self-esteem sank even lower, but she never mentioned it to her mom. At thirteen, she was still a virgin, but this would change along with her behavior. Over the course of one summer, she'd gone from a little girl in need of her father, to the talk of all the young boys around her neighborhood, known as *the trailer trash flipper*. Paris began running away for days at a time and it was around this time that her promiscuity grew worst.

Venturing out, she found her way to the north side of town. She had a black friend named Felicia from school who lived on 32nd and Cherry, which was in the heart of the ghetto. Felicia had an older brother Sammy, a self proclaimed pimp, who immediately recognized the vulnerability in her, she was completely mesmerized by him. Sammy would talk to her for hours about her problems and when she turned fourteen he even bought her a present. This was the first time in her life that anybody, other that her mother, had shown any concern for her. She loved Sammy, and no one could tell her that he didn't love her back. So when he asked her to turn her first trick *for them*, Paris didn't give it a second thought. She'd been giving herself away for free anyhow, now she had the man of her dreams and would do whatever was necessary to keep him loving her. Unfortunately for her, this would be the beginning of an everlasting cycle she'd continue to repeat

* * * * *

When they made it back Venus and Kimmie were laughing and joking as they came through the door, they'd hit it off right away. Agent Chan had done everything she could to make them as comfortable as possible. She'd gotten out to help with their bags, offered them the front seat, complemented them on their looks, etc.

"I think I like this bitch already, daddy where you find her at?" Venus said at one point during their drive.

Key thought she was being a little too nice, but he figured she was just trying to be accepted by her senior wife-in-laws.

Paris and Chrissy were in the living room when they came in. Chrissy rose from the couch with a smile bright enough to turn midnight into day.

"Hey, daddy's been telling us all about y'all. How was Reno, I never been there," she said.

"Awh, girl, it was beautiful and them tricks out there ain't cheap so that made it even better," Classy said.

"What kind of style is this? It's nice," she said to Venus playing with her hair.

"It's something new they wearing out there. The style alone was three hundred. Key looked at her.

"Three hundred?"

"Yeah, daddy, don't you think it was worth it? All my clients loved it."

"For three hundred muthafuckin' dollars they betta' had loved it," he said grinning. Normally he would've check one of his hoes for spending his money so recklessly, but this bitch had just hit him with twenty-five bands upon arrival, not to mention the seventeen they sent prior to coming home.

Fuck it, the hoe earned it, he thought to himself as he walked off leaving the girls to themselves.

Paris was in her own world pretending to pay them no attention. He stopped by the couch.

"What's up with you and all this monkey shit you been on lately? I'm about ten seconds from putting you in a coma bitch. Take yo' punk ass in there and get acquainted, the world don't revolved around yo' nasty ass." She got up. "And I promise you, this my last time talking," he said, walking upstairs.

She rolled her eyes and dragged her feet to the other room.

"What's wrong with this hoe?" Venus said with a funny look.

"She wants some dick," Chrissy blurted out. They all giggled.

"Is that it? Bitch, join the club. You'll get used to it and besides, dick ain't everything, keep yo' mind on his money," Venus had automatically assumed the leadership role within the flock. She felt like it was her duty. Key didn't have to tell her this, she was seasoned enough to know that it was her job to keep the other hoes minds on track when Key wasn't around.

Paris almost fixed her mouth to ask her if he'd given her any, but decided to wait until they were alone to ask a question like that. They barely knew each other and she didn't want to offend her by putting Venus on the spot in that way.

Venus reached into her Gucci purse and pulled out a small black plastic bag tossing it to Paris.

"Here, this might help you, its done wonders for me." Paris looked into the bag and instantly began to laugh. "What is it girl?"

Chrissy said reaching. And when she pulled out the dildo and a picture of Key everybody laughed uncontrollably.

"Nawh, I'm cool, a bitch need some heat behind that shit, baby," Paris said.

"Okay, suit yourself," Venus said placing the articles back into her purse. "Anybody else? Going once…" "Girl, you crazy," Chrissy said laughing still.

"Nawh, this bitch the crazy one, I know how to take care of my needs."

Chan noticed that Venus and Classy had a Q inside of a heart tattooed on their necks. This would be her conversation piece to begin the inquiry into Quesha's murder. Key had already explained to her what the Q represented so she knew that asking them a second time could raise a red flag. Patience was a skill that the bureau hammered into all personnel training for deep cover operations. The moment would come it always did.

* * * * *

Later on that night at The Empire Room the VIP was packed with your usual ballers, from Milwaukee Bucks players to young thousandaire's holding down blocks.

Key and Red happened to be the only pimps in the place. They were a rare breed; especially for their age range, most niggas in their generation couldn't begin to phantom the idea of what it must have been like to walk in their shoes. They were well educated in the field of dealing with women, and preferred to be men instead of taking on the sucka's mentality that niggas seemed to have adopted, an epidemic that had spread throughout the country. *It ain't trickin' if you got it,* a term coined by new wave rappers. And since most young cats tend to do their best to emulate the videos in search of an identity they think that whatever the rappers say is law.

But Key and Red had the privilege of hearing and seeing the truth. So they could weed through that garbage and knew that most rappers were a bunch of simple-minded dudes who were no different than their idiot followers.

They sat at the bar and discussed ideas and went over details of how they wanted to run their club versus the way other establishments were run. The girls were in the back with several bottles of open champagne on the table. The liquor had long since taken over them all except Chan; she'd been sipping on the same glass for the past two hours. Venus had the floor as usual.

"How many of you hoes can rake in twenty stacks in one month with ease?" she said. Apple raised her glass up high.

"Try twenty-five, baby. And I ain't talking no one month out of the year on a fluke shit either," she said slapping fives with Hennessey; one of Red's new bootys.

"A fluke, honey never, you know how I gets down. You done seen a hoe at work. That's why this is decked out in over ten Gs," she said sticking out her right hand showing off a slew of diamond rings.

"Yeah, my daddy's more than proud to have me. Fuck *America's Top Model*, I'm America's Top Whore."

Everyone at the table busted out into laughter.

Apple nearly spit her drink out. "Girl, if you don't sit yo' drunk ass down."

"As a matter of fact, let's make a toast." "Not to your crazy ass we ain't," Chan said.

"Shut yo' ass up, Kimmie, nawh not to me. I wanna make a toast to the best hoe I ever knew. My baby Quesha, she saved me from that bum ass nigga and was a real bitch."

They all stood up and toasted.

"May you rest in peace, baby. I love you girl," Venus said looking above. She was emotional and crying now. Classy went over to wrap her arm around Venus.

"She was too young girl, I miss her," Venus said with her head on Classy's shoulder touching the memorial "Q" on her neck.

"I know baby, but ain't nothing we can do."

Chan was observing as they walked off toward the ladies room.

"Who was that girl she was talking about?" Hennessey said to Apple.

"A good friend and a bad bitch," she said as she rose up to join them.

When she walked in Venus was wiping her face. "You okay, girl?"

"Yeah, I'm alright, Apple, thanks."

They talked for a few minutes about happy moments they shared with Quesha when they were all in New Orleans together. When Venus was finished fixing her makeup they went back to join the others.

"Come on y'all, let's go take some pictures," Chrissy said grabbing her glass.

As they walked past the bar Key gestured for Classy to stop by him. He'd been watching what was going on at their table.

"What's wrong wit' Venus?"

"She was just thinking about Quesha, plus, she been drinking, baby; she's okay."

"Alright, make sure you watch her."

"You know I will," she said then kissed him on the cheek.

When Classy walked away Red was ready to start a roasting session. "I see you getting kissed on the jaw in shit nigga, wipe yo' cheek homie you got lipstick on it."

"Man, you know how hoes get with that alcohol in their system," he said wiping his face with a napkin. "Is it gone?"

"Yeah, you good."

While the pictures were developing they loitered around the area, ignoring every nigga who came of the wood works to shoot his shot.

Chan was talking to Venus about Quesha when he seemed to appear out of nowhere. Chrissy spotted him first, but before she was able to pull Paris's coat he was already two steps in back of her.

"So, this what you two hoes been doing? Partying! I've been searching high and low for you two bitches."

Looking at him now Paris said, "What's up?" And turned back around eyeballing Chrissy as if she wanted to say, "Why the hell you ain't tell me he was walking up bitch?"

He grabbed her by the hair. "Bitch, don't turn your back on me."

By this time everybody was aware of what was taking place.

"Profit let her go," Chrissy said rushing over to help as Paris struggled to get free.

"I don't know who the hell you are, nigga, but you betta' let my girl go," Classy said pulling a knife out of her purse. He released her hair and started walking toward Classy until he suddenly felt the barrel of a gun pressing up against his back.

"Take another step and I'ma empty this muthafucka in yo' kidney," Venus said, moving to the side of him. No one knew she had a gun out except for Chan.

He stopped for a split second then tried to turn and grab the barrel of the 380 caliber. But before he could make a full spin, Chan had already anticipated his actions. She grabbed his right arm swinging his body toward her as she landed a single solid blow to his groin. It all happened in a flash, by the time Key and Red made it to the area it was over and security were picking him up off the floor.

"What happened?" Key said.

"He was tryna put his hands on Paris so we had to get with 'em," Venus said, putting her purse back under her arm.

Key was looking at Chan wondering where she learned those moves.

"What! My dad sent me to martial arts classes for five years. I still remember some of the shit," she said.

"Let's get outta here," he said. "That's enough of this shit for one night."

* * * * *

On the way home, everybody praised Chan for her quick thinking and skills.

"Kimmie, girl you turned into Jackie Chan on that nigga."

Hearing her real last name brought her closer to reality. She was glad that the situation hadn't gone any further. Her whole purpose of subduing him was to make sure of that. And she was pissed that all of it had to happen just as she had Venus talking about Quesha.

Key was driving listening to everything the girls were talking about in the backseat. For some reason he was beginning to think that the bitch

Kimmie was too perfect. He didn't buy her story about the martial arts classes. *But where else could she have learned that shit, the police academy or some shit. No, what the hell the police gonna be doing sending somebody at me, I'm pimping now, I gotta be tripping.* He wasn't even sure they did shit like that to pimps. And after a few minutes he stopped wrestling with the idea.

Chapter 17

When Key woke up that morning, he barely had room to turn onto his side. They all piled into his bed after he was already asleep. He squeezed his way through the half naked bodies and headed to the bathroom.

When he came out his cell phone was ringing, it was Red.

"Top of the morning, Player."

Red had obviously been up early. Key wondered how he did it. He hadn't drunk a thing and was tired and this nigga was killing XO all night.

"Nothing, just getting up."

"Them hoes musta' wore you out last night nigga?"

"Nawh, that's you with them orgies, I keeps it P."

"Yeah, whatever, check this out though. I think some niggas was following me last night man."

"What make you think that?"

"Well, when we left the club I saw a black Intrepid with tinted windows in my rearview. I didn't pay it no attention, but when I got to the hotel I seen the same car ride past. And whoever was in it slowed down like they were checking me out."

"So what you do?"

"What you think I did, I went in the hotel what else could I do."

"You sure yo' ass wasn't drunk?"

"Man that lil shit didn't do nothing to me you know I can handle my liquor." Key knew he right, last night was just another day for Red.

"Have I ever cried wolf to you, nigga?" Red said.

"I believe you, dawg, but they were probably just some niggas tryna hit a quick lick. I wouldn't sweat it too much."

"I'm not I was just telling you because the shit tripped me out homie. But what was up wit' yo' Chinese bitch with the Lucy Lu stunts in shit? Nigga, that shit was hilarious. Man, my hoes laughed all the way to the hotel," Red said laughing.

Key even found it humorous.

"Yeah, you see the way she got on his ass nigga! I'm protected like the President."

"Haha, I wouldn't get that chick mad if I was you. I wonder where she learned that shit at though, I might send my bitches there," Red said still laughing.

"I don't know, but a nigga betta' watch out," Key said laughing.

Chan was the first to get up.

"What you watching?" she said flopping on the couch. "*ESPN*, I'm surprised you up."

"You know I don't drink like that, them hoes still knocked out from that liquor."

That was another thing that got to him; Key had yet to meet a hooker who didn't drink. But she was a fresh turnout, so maybe that was her excuse.

"You have fun kickin' ass last night," he said jokingly.

"Yeah, that did feel kinda good hitting him in the nuts," she said laughing. She actually enjoyed her night out with the other girls. Chan hadn't done that in a while, her real life was rather boring. They were all cool and she genuinely felt a sense of sorrow for what she was doing, something that had never happened to her during a case.

They talked for a while until the business phone rang. It was a client for her.

"That was one of my regulars, baby, I gotta get ready so I can go get you this money," she said.

Key's mind wouldn't rest; he kept getting a gut feeling that something just wasn't right about Kimmie he needed a second opinion and decided to see T.A.

* * * * *

When he got over to his place, they sat at the table where the chess board was set up.

"What's on your mind homie?" T.A. said waiting on Key's opening move.

"It's my Chinese chick. Man, something is bothering with this dame."

"Like what I thought you said she was one of your best people?" T.A. said calculating his next three moves.

Key told him about last night and all the other things that had been bothering him. Then when he mentioned her possibly being planted by the police for some reason T.A.
began to laugh.

"Why you laughing? I'm serious T."

"I'm sorry, homie, but that don't make no sense. The broad's been breaking bread with you for a while now. And the police wouldn't waste all that time and energy just to bust you, dawg; that just ain't gone happen. You paranoid, lil pimpin', take it easy."

He was about to move, but stopped to think for a second.

"Now, I'll tell you who would try to pull some shit like that, the Feds. But in yo' case I highly doubt it, they normally do that to niggas who they want really bad. Especially when they fuckin' with kids in shit. You ain't been doing that have you?" he looked at Key.

"Nawh, man. I make sure all my people grown."

"Good, well I doubt that then."

"So the Feds will come at a nigga for pimpin'?"

"Hell yeah, it's called Interstate Trafficking. But in your case, they'd have much more cause this bitch all the way in yo' business P. This is nonsense though; besides, ain't she been on dates and shit?"

"Yeah."

"Well, there you go, and I'm sure your other people have seen her in action right?" Key shook his head *no*.

"That still don't mean shit, have you at least fucked the bitch yet?"

Key shook his head *no* again.

"Say, pimp, I know you got a reputation to protect, but this me...you ain't gone tell me you haven't test drove that piece at least once, nigga?" T.A. gave him a look as though he didn't believe him.

"I'm serious, dawg. I ain't touched her and the crazy thing is she don't seem to mind either." T.A. leaned back and looked at him.

"Yeah, that is odd. But them your two options and if the bitch is *them* people it would be unethical for her to do either one. I can't believe you actually got me entertaining this shit. I personally think you tripping. But I'll tell you one thing, if you right, your ass is already screwed, lil player. And guess what else?"

"What?"

"Checkmate nigga, get yo' game up."

* * * * *

Chan was meeting with S.A. Bender after Greg Daley reviewed the recording of Key and Red's conversation he reported to his superior to fill him in.

"What happened last night, Chan?" Bender was watering some plants when she came into his office.

"What do you mean, sir?"

"Well, our recordings picked up a conversation with two of the subjects were discussing you being involved in a brawl of some sort," he was sitting down now.

"Well, sir I had no choice, one of the girls had a gun…"

"What?"

"Yes, there was a situation with one of the other girls' ex-pimp and…"

He cut her off. "Stop there, I don't need to hear anymore. I just had to make sure you were okay. How's the investigation going?"

"It's going well, sir; actually, I had Venus talking about the victim when the incident happened, so that kind of screwed me. But I'm confident it will be fruitful."

"That's good news then; you're free to go just try to stay away from anymore confrontations if you can help it agent. I'd hate to blow all the good work you guys have been doing on this."

* * * * *

When she made it back to the house, Key was already there. He was trying to study her moves to see if he could sniff out any lies.

"You made it back. That was a long date, you left before I did," he was looking to see her physical reactions.

"Yeah, I know, baby, he wanted me to stay longer. He said something about his wife being out of town," she said, handing Key a thousand dollars.

He wasn't convinced. "That's what I'm talking about. Aye, I want you to take a ride with me somewhere."

"Oh, okay. You ready now?" She was puzzled but had to play along.

"Yeah, I'm ready, but don't you wanna freshen up first?"

She was getting nervous now. But Chan was way too skilled to show it.

"Oh no, baby, I didn't have to do anything. He just likes to talk and sometimes he might want to cop an occasional feel," she said, impressing herself with the way she was able to roll the lies off her tongue. Her answer was the one Key had anticipated. He gave her a slight smile.

"Okay, let's go then."

On the way down the stairs her mind was racing trying to figure out his angle. *Had he seen me at the bureau building, was someone following me, does he know who I am?* She couldn't figure it out. And when he asked her did she have the keys to her apartment, she knew that something had to be wrong.

Think quick, Li she said to herself. "No, baby, I left them in the house." They were in the car now.

"I almost forgot didn't I have a set?" he asked looking at her.

"Yeah, I remember giving them to you."

* * * * *

The apartment they had set up for her wasn't far from Key's place. It was a short ride and on the way she was trying to make sure there was nothing that could reveal her identity, there wasn't.

The inside was arranged to perfection she had brought several items from home; mainly a lot of pictures, clothing, and feminine products. Anyone who visited would actually believe that she lived there, and for the past few months she did. Acting on the advice of her supervisor, she'd hadn't been home since the first day of her initial contact with Key.

She was still wondering why they were there, and she became relieved when Key took a seat on the sofa. She turned the TV on and sat next to him.

"Baby, why we come over here? Did I do something wrong that we need to discuss?"

He wanted to say, *Wrong, no bitch, that's the whole issue here you never do nothing wrong!* but instead he finessed the situation. Placing her hand in his he said, "No, baby, you ain't did nothing wrong, I just wanted to spend some time with you."

When he reached for her hand, she nearly pulled back out of instinct. But Chan remembered the reason she was here, it was just a little physical contact, nothing serious. She stared at him with a blank look.

"Is something wrong with me taking the time out to appreciate you?"

He was reading her every move.

"Of course not, but why me out of all the others?" her answer sounded like she was dodging, but he went forward with his mission.

"You know, after last night I feel like it's the least I could do. If you hadn't been there, I'm not sure how that would've turned out. Not to mention the fact that you didn't freeze up."

"I just did what I had to do. I couldn't let anybody get hurt if I could help it."

"Yeah, I know and I appreciate that. Come here."

Not knowing what else to do she got up and sat on his lap. This was a situation that she had gone over in her mind, but never knew how she would handle it. And now here she was faced with the inevitable.

"I got you something."

He reached in his pocket and pulled out a black box. And her heart nearly skipped a beat when she saw the diamond tennis bracelet. This was the first time anyone had ever given her anything of this magnitude. Her first reaction was to kiss and hug him, which she did. Something that wasn't an act, and when she realized what she'd done it was too late.

As he laid her back on the couch, Chan began to come out of the trance. Out of nervousness, she began shaking. Her face displayed a look of fear, confusion, and willingness all in one.

Key was certain that any second now she was going to find a way to stop the proceedings. And in her mind she nearly did.

"This can't happen, what are you doing, Li you're on the job, this whole case will go down the tubes." She had a million thoughts running through her mind.

It wasn't right, but she was only human. And when he entered her, every thought that occupied her mind disappeared.

Key was for sure now that his calculations had been incorrect. But figured he'd may as well enjoy the moment. After twenty minutes of them wrestling on the couch, she wanted to go into the bedroom. They went at it for another hour, with her completely letting go. He fucked her pussy and mouth one after the other and she took in each repetition, eagerly inviting the next.

When they finished Key went straight to the bathroom. She laid there gazing at the ceiling thinking of what she'd just done. There was no way this could be explained to her boss, or her partner. The only explanation she could conjure up to use was that she didn't want to blow her cover, what would he have thought had she not gone along with it. Yes, that's what she'd say to her superiors, grand jury, and at trial if need be. Chan knew that she could face serious consequences if this got out. But the funny thing was that she didn't seem to care.

When Key came back in the room he was putting his pants back on, and she found herself looking at him wishing they could do it again. But those thoughts were interrupted.

"You getting dressed or what?"

She snapped out of it and headed for the bathroom.

Key was adjusting his shirt in the mirror. *This bitch can't be what I thought she was, not after all that.* He smiled at himself. "They can't find a young nigga of my pedigree nowhere on this side of the world. I see why that bitch been bringing me all that cold hard cash. I'm definitely on my way to seeing a meal ticket."

They didn't go straight home when they left. Key wanted to reiterate a few important points while he bent some corners, kind of like renewing her pledge of allegiance to his P.

After stopping for beverages he headed to his old neighborhood.

"You know, baby, this is where it all started. I used to run around these blocks doing every kinda hustle under the sun, me and my main man Red. Most of the people around here will never know what it's like to get away from this hood, let alone drive a Benz like we're doing right now. Some of 'em comfortable the way they are and out of the ones who aren't only a hand full of them got enough guts to do something about it. But not me, I'd rather die before I live a life of mediocrity. Muthafuckas be scared to take chances because they fear the consequences of getting caught. But police and the DA can go suck a horse dick, I'ma live the way I want to 'til I check out, and it won't be to no penitentiary either."

When he said that, she looked into Key's eyes and could see that he was dead serious.

He seen a crowd of young kids walking up the street and pulled over waving them to the car.

"You see them? This used to be me growing up, baby."

Rolling down the window as they approached he could hear the compliments toward the Benz.

"How y'all doing?"

They didn't even hear his question, the car had their one hundred percent attention.

"Man, where you get a car like this?"

"Stop asking stupid questions you know he gotta be ballin'."

"I'ma have me a car like this one day," another one said before Key cut in.

"Forget the car, where y'all on the way to?" he said.

"The store right up here," he had to be the youngest out of the group.

Key reached into his pocket and peeled off several twenty dollar bills handing one to each of them.

"Thanks, man; what's yo' name?" the tallest of the crew said.

"Keyshawn...aye, y'all be smooth. And big man, take care of these little ones."

When he pulled away he looked in the rearview mirror for a few seconds. "Me and you come from two different walks of life baby and I'm sure you didn't see shit like that when you were coming up right?" She shook her head *no*.

"You know why, cause people outside the ghetto don't live in desperation. Only in a ghetto will you see some shit like that, muthafuckas around here love to see a nigga like me cause it gives them hope, especially lil' kids. They feel like if he can make something happen from a bad situation so can I. Every day is a struggle for most families around here and those kids don't know right now, but one day the burden will be on them. Maybe even sooner than later, that's why every chance I get I stop to give them words of encouragement."

As he proceeded toward the highway, Chan was looking out the window at the beaten down houses. She really admired his sense of compassion for other people and for a second tried to imagine what life must've been like coming from where he did. She clutched the bracelet on her wrist and wished to God that circumstances had been different with them. He was saying something, but Chan was in deep thought.

"Kimmie, you hear what I said?"

"No, baby, I'm sorry what was that?" he tapped her arm.

"I said, I'm shooting for a million…you wit' me?" "Yeah, I'm with you, daddy." And she meant every word.

* * * * *

When they arrived back to the house all the girls were up and ready for work. Calls came in at all times of the day, but the afternoon and late night hours were the busiest.

Venus was the first to notice the bracelet. She grabbed Chan's arm. "Damn, girl, I like this, you wanna swap it for something else?"

"Nawh, I love it, wouldn't trade it for nothing in the world."

Venus was slightly jealous, but the bracelet didn't amount to half the jewelry she had.

Paris was hot when she came into the living room and seen Venus examining Kimmie's wrist.

After one look at the thing she left the room. Key had allowed her to buy plenty of clothes, but had yet to award her with any jewelry.

They all wondered where Key had taken her so early, but no one dared to question him or his whereabouts, to do so would call for swift penalties. They knew better, but would get it out of Kimmie the first chance they got.

When Key stepped out of the bathroom after taking a shower Paris was going into the bedroom and mumbled something under her breath.

"What you say, bitch?" he'd had it with her.

"I said, what makes that bitch so special? I know I've bought my way in to get that same treatment or whatever else y'all went to do," she said looking him up and down. Key couldn't believe what he was hearing. He palmed her face and rammed the back of her head against the wall.

"Bitch, you musta' lose yo' stupid ass mind. The only thing for sale around here is you hoe, you can't buy me, bitch," he slapped her to the floor. "And I'm not your business fag, it's the other way around."

When he kicked her in the stomach she tried to catch her breath while holding up a hand as if she was trying to speak, but couldn't. He grabbed her hand then broke he pinky finger. Yelling out in agony she said, "Please, daddy, I'm sorry."

"I should break everyone of these fucking fingers."

"No, please."

Her words brought him back to his senses and he tossed her hand to the ground.

"Venus," he yelled down the stairs. She was up there in a heartbeat.

"Yes."

"Clean this bitch up and take her to get that finger checked out," he said before slamming the door to his room.

Venus walked down the hallway; Paris was still lying on the floor holding her hand softly crying. She kneeled down next to her shaking her head. "Girl, I told you...let me see your hand." She sat up.

"Come on...get up so I can take you to the ER."

* * * * *

They made it back to find the other girls were gone, they were all working. It couldn't have been fifteen minutes before the phone rang. It was a customer requesting three girls.

"Call Classy and tell her to meet y'all there when she's done," he told Venus.

Paris was in no mood for work. "Daddy can I stay back, I'm sorry. I just wanna lie down for a few hours."

"What! You gotta be fuckin' nuts. You cost me enough money today. Ain't nothing wrong with your pussy," he said with a grim look on his face.

Chapter 18

The Grand Opening of Allure was on schedule. T.A. had the contractors separate the club into four sections that made a T shape. The Black room was in the front just past the main entrance. The Gold and Platinum rooms were to the east and west, with The Palace being located in the back. Each room was painted, designed, and furnished in its name in color. The Palace was white and burgundy. Since it was the smallest in size they decided it would be VIP.

T.A. monitored the entrance while Key and Red worked the floor from room to room making sure their employees ran the club smoothly.

The stage was being prepped for a performance by Riffic, a local hip hop artist who was hot on the Milwaukee rap scene. They toyed with the idea of bringing in a national artist, but in the end settled on someone who was repin' The-Mil.

Special Agent Collins was at work doing his investigating. He was doing most of the work on Red for Chicago's field office. The young, twenty-nine-year-old black agent still had the fresh face to blend in with any unsuspecting crowd. Walking through the place from front to back, he memorized the entire layout, making a special note to remember an office the three partners had set-up adjacent to the VIP section. He estimated that the costs of the place from renovations to interior decorating had to be in the tens of thousands. Not to mention the five thousand that was paid to the local alderman to pull some strings with the zoning committee to allow renovations without a board vote. A procedure that was meant to only be used in situations where renovations would not change the capacity limits to the establishment.

The agency had three incriminating conversations recorded from wiretaps on T.A.'s cell phone with him and Alderman Jonathan Billings. They discussed the services the alderman would provide and payment for his role in getting the project to go through. At one point the alderman was quoted as saying, "That's my district T and whatever the fuck I want to happen around there will happen, with or without the committee's blessings. And I can guarantee that you stay open long enough to see a major return on your investment. Shit, I don't care if you have girls running through there butt ass naked. Just make sure I get me some.".

After carefully reviewing the conversations, the F.B.I. opened an investigation on the alderman for charges of corruption of a public official, accepting bribes, and abuse of authority by a public official.

By 12:30, the club was well over capacity and there was still a line that extended past the building. T.A. instructed the doorman to go outside and announce that the cover charge was now fifty dollars and a hundred if anyone wanted to bypass the line.

Key and Red were watching Riffic's performance when T.A. finally found them after searching through the crowd for fifteen minutes.

"That nigga, Smoove, just came in here about a half hour ago," he said speaking directly into Key's ear just loud enough to be heard over the music.

Key looked at him, then tapped Red on the shoulder gesturing him toward the office. And when they got inside, Key was the first one to say something.

"I can't believe that nigga had the nerve to show up here."

"Did he come in with anybody?" Red said.

"No, he didn't see me either. I was in the collection room grabbing some of the cash to put in the safe. Which reminds me, we doing excellent numbers at the door and they still coming" he said smiling.

Key wasn't paying any attention; he wanted to do something gruesome to Smoove and he was playing the scene out in his mind.

"What's up, baby; you alright?" Red said.

"I'm good my nigga" he was trying to appear as though he wasn't affected by Smoove showing up, but he clearly was and they both could see it.

"Fuck that nigga man, he ain't no P. he's a sucka; the game gone serve him for that hating ass move he pulled," T.A. said. But Key really wasn't trying to hear it. He knew that T.A. was only saying that because it hadn't happened to him. Had the shoe been on the other foot T.A. would've been ready for blood and all three of them knew this to be a fact.

They changed the subject matter on to business; going over everything that worked and didn't work in terms of their initial plans of operation. After talking a few more minutes, they left the office getting back to their duties.

Agent Collins watched as they exited the office while he talked to a female patron as a cover.

Before they could make it past the dance floor near the area where the stage was setup Smoove was walking toward them. He put a big plastic smile on his face as they approached.

"What's up, young players? I heard about y'all lil grand opening so you know I had to come check it out."

Nobody said a word; Key had to restrain himself from cracking him upside the head with something. But he promised his partners that he'd play it cool. Neither one of them wanted to spoil their opening night, not even Key. They had a good thing on their hands and acting off emotion or impulse could screw all that up.

T.A. was trying to read him to see what his intentions were when Red began to speak.

"Yeah, you know real Player's do real shit" he said emphasizing the word *real*. "And we leave them sucka moves open for these busters to make."

Smoove knew what he was getting at. And he was pleased to know that what he'd done was still fresh on their minds. He didn't give a hoot that he'd come there alone. He prided himself and his career on being a one man show and using bully type tactics to navigate his way through any situation that entailed a weak opponent.

"Tell me about it, like that coward move you pulled on me when I went to jail right?" he was looking at Red with pure hatred in his eyes.

"Come on man, you still mad about them hoes you lost down there nigga. We put 'em to good use you should be proud of a nigga, Smoove." Red was antagonizing him. Smoove wanted to fuck him up right then, but knew that was a risky move seeing as though he was in their element.

"You lil niggas ain't no true Ps, cause if ya' was, I'd had a chance at getting my hoes back," he glanced at Key then said to T.A., "What's up with yo' protégés? I thought you were raising some stomp down niggas?"

Key was about to say something but T.A. cut him off.

"Say, man, why you gotta come up in our shit disrespecting my niggas? Personally, I think both of 'em are much better players than you claim to be. You made that bullshit move on my nigga, Key, here cause you got knocked for some funky ass hoes?! A certified mack woulda' chalked that shit up and kept it pimpin'."

Smoove fixed his mouth to say something, but T.A. held up a hand.

"Look, man, why don't you just enjoy yourself tonight. Go over there to the bartender and tell her to give you a bottle of Moet on the house and let's bury this shit."

Smoove was caught completely off guard by T.A.'s kindness and when he stuck his hand out, Smoove felt obligated to shake it. The man had been a true gentleman and his words seemed genuine.

When they shook hands, Key couldn't believe T.A., he felt like he was down playing the violation that Smoove had committed against him. And when Smoove turned to shake his hand he said, "Nigga, I ain't shaking yo' muthafuckin' hand, you wanna talk about a coward move, that was a real one you made, chump. If you had a beef with me you shoulda' came to see me."

He was about to keep going when T.A. put his hand on his shoulder.

"You gotta understand that my nigga's angry Smoove, baby. But it's all cool, man; just get that bottle, homie and enjoy the rest of the night. As a matter of fact enjoy what I call the fruit of a hoe's labor," he said, waving both arms around the place. Smoove walked away and headed for the bar.

"Aye, man I know we tryna' keep it cool in all for business purposes, but I think you went a little over board shaking that fag's hand in shit T," Key was heated.

"Are you done?" T.A. said, giving him a cool look. "Let's go back here for a second."

As they headed toward the office, Agent Collins wondered what was going on. He was well trained at not only reading body languages but in lip reading also. The body language and demeanor that Key was giving off said that there was definitely a problem and since he was channeling all of this toward Smoove he figured it was with him. He made attempts to read their lips, but too many people were moving between them blocking his view. Whatever it was, it didn't concern him, he was here to do surveillance on the three partners.

When they got back in the office T.A. went straight to the land line and dialed a number. A male voice answered.

"Suit up and come up to the club, call me when you get outside. Pull up next to the back door." He hung up. "You gotta learn how to control your emotions, my nigga; you actually think I was on some peace shit with that nigga after all that slick shit he was talking?" Key suddenly felt kind of silly.

"It ain't what you do to a nigga, it's how you do it. That nigga totally off balance cause I used this," he said pointing to his head.

"Let's get back out here fella's, we got a business to run," he said smiling.

When they came out, T.A. went straight over to the bar where Smoove was at. He wanted to keep a close eye on him until he got the call. Red and Key were his lil brothers and this nigga had to be stupid if he thought he would get away with disrespecting them like that, especially in his face.

Key strolled around the front wondering what T.A. was up to he knew that whatever it was it would be fatal. In all the years he had known T.A. He had never gone against him and he always tried his best to protect him and Red from making any stupid moves that could possibly land them in prison because they weren't using their heads. He thought of all the things they had dodged because of T.A., even times when he had stuck his own neck out there for them. T.A. was a real friend to them both. A term that many used but few knew what it really meant.

Smoove had always been impressed with T.A., he'd met him when he was teenager and knew then that he was way ahead of his time. He was nearly fifteen years his senior and yet as they sat at the bar chopping game you couldn't tell. They were laughing and joking about times that they had run into one another on the road in different states and cities. But in the back of his mind Smoove knew that T.A.'s loyalty lay with his two cronies. He was well aware of his background and the type of breed that he descended from. The more they talked, Smoove was able to see through the charade that he was possibly putting on.

"Man, you being so nice to me, nigga; shit, if a muthafucka didn't know it, he'd think I was your partner and not yo' two workers up there."

He was fishing for some kind of sign, but T.A. was as sharp as fresh razor and let the comment go right over his head.

He laughed. "Smoove, you gotta take it easy on the young niggas they the future of this shit," he said referring to Key and Red.

"Nawh, you the future, I don't know about them two phonies," T.A. was tired of talking to him by now and wanted to put a bullet in his fat mouth himself. But just as he was about to say something he felt his phone vibrating. Looking at the screen he could see that it was the magic call he'd been waiting for.

"Excuse me, homie, I'll be right back," he said smiling.

Smoove didn't like the smile he gave him and at this point knew that he had something cooking. So when T.A. came back he thanked him for his hospitality and said that he had to get going; assuring him that he'd come back to patronize them again.

Key was behind the Gold room when T.A. came over and ordered a single shot of Remy Martin. He turned the shot up and downed it all at once.

"Damn, that shot hit the spot," he winked at Key and went back to work.

As soon as he seen Smoove almost at the door he pulled out his cell and called that same number back again. When he heard the man pick up he pushed the end button.

On the other end the man knew that was the signal that their target was on the way out. The two men in the black Ford Taurus waited patiently as he started up the brown Cadillac DTS and pulled into traffic. The driver let him get almost a block away before he took off behind him.

"Just pull up on the side of him and I'ma do him right there," the man in the passenger seat said.

"He wants it done as far away from the club as possible, relax man."

Dressed in all black, heavily armed they both had plastic Uzi's with sixty round clips."

After Smoove pulled off he checked his rearview constantly then several blocks later relaxed thinking that he might have misjudged T.A., either that or he had left too fast for him to summon anybody up there to do anything.

They had been following him for about two minutes now and decide that they were far enough away from the club to carry out their mission.

"Speed up a lil' bit and get me on the side of his car."

When Smoove seen the Taurus coming toward him at a high rate of speed he didn't think much of it; figuring it was probably just some drunk person leaving enough space between him and the car in front of his to be able to pull off just in case it was something funny going on. The passenger window was completely down and the shooter was in position. Smoove was looking in the driver's door mirror when the car made it to him. The car came to a sudden halt and by the time he tried to make his getaway it was too late. He was hit multiple times within a matter of seconds with blood splattering everywhere. And when the passenger saw him slump over to his side he leaned out of the car window and nearly emptied the clip into his face and chest before the driver took off.

"Is he dead?"

He laughed and said, "Is he dead?! Nigga, that's like asking me did I just shot him. Of course he's dead. Hurry up and drop me off I gotta get to the hospital I'm about to have a son any minute now," he said nonchalantly, as if what he'd just done was nothing more than a day at the office.

Chapter 19

By mid-afternoon, Smoove's murder had sent shockwaves throughout the entire city. It wasn't so much the murder itself that people were talking about, because Milwaukee had its fair share of homicides each year. But the manner in which he'd been slain. He was struck eighteen times. And with six bullets to his face a mortician would have a rough job putting it back together.

On the news at noon, they released his name and flashed a picture during the coverage of the story. Chan, Venus, and Classy were in the exercise room working out. Venus and Classy moved closer to the TV when his photo hit the screen.

Chan could tell that they obviously knew him by the way they looked at one another.

They were showing clips of footage that was taken earlier that morning. The reporter was talking with a homicide detective.

"A witness called 911 at about 2:00 a.m. and said that the victim was driving alongside this busy street, he pulled over and a white vehicle came by speeding and suddenly stopped right on the side of him. Then the passenger shot several times into the vehicle," the Caucasian detective said.

The reporter was asking about the make and model of the assassin's car. As the camera man panned over to the Cadillac that was riddled with bullets, Classy put her hand over her mouth.

"Fuck that pink ass nigga, that's what his ass gets," Venus said, walking over to the treadmill.

"They fucked him up," Chan said looking at the screen. "You must've known him, girl?"

"Yeah, we knew his weak ass, fuck him, Kimmie. I don't wanna talk about dude."

Before she began running, Venus placed her hand on her neck.

It was at that moment when Chan got a strong hunch that Smoove must have been Quesha's killer. The only time Venus unconsciously touched the tattoo was when she thought about her. So, why was she thinking about her now after seeing the story about this man's murder? Chan needed to find out who he was and she also wanted to know why they were so angry with him.

* * * * *

Before she could get dressed Chan got a call. And by the name and location that was given to Paris she knew that Bender wanted her at the office for an emergency meeting.

When she arrived Morgan informed her that they were waiting on her in conference room A.

Chan opened the door to find Bender, Collins, and Daley discussing Smoove's murder.

"Ah, there she is."

For some reason her boss was in a good mood today.

There were mug shots of Smoove, whose real name was Tyrone White.

Collins was talking. "As I was saying, I could tell that there was some tension between this gentleman and one of our subjects."

"Which one?" Bender said, scanning some papers.

"Keyshawn, sir…and I find it odd that he was killed right after he left."

"Just one moment," Bender said to him. "I want to fill Chan in on where we are here."

Turning to her he began with Collins. "As you know, Agents Collins, here was covering the opening of their club last night. Well, he noticed that our subjects were interacting with this man here," he pointed to a picture of Smoove. "Initially, he didn't think much of it until he watches the news this morning and saw that this very man had been killed shortly after leaving this location."

Chan was suddenly starting to feel lightheaded and nauseated. She had been experiencing this for the past week. And for the past two days, was beginning to wonder what it was.

"This morning he runs that name through the database and discovers that the guy has rap sheets in four states with
the latest one being in…"

"Let me guess...New Orleans?" Chan said, rubbing her neck.

"Are you alright?" Bender had been noticing her discomfort for the past five minutes.

"Yes, I'm fine, sir."

"You don't look fine, agent."

"I'm okay, sir; what were you saying?" he gave her an odd look.

"Okay, where was I? Oh, yes...turns out the guy had been arrested down there on a felony gun charge and I believe some drugs as well. Jail records show that he was in custody for three weeks and was released a couple of days before Watson's girl was murdered. Chan was reading the file and when he said that she looked up.

"We don't have anything concrete, but based on all the information that we do have I think there's a strong possibility that he had something to do with her murder. Thus, explaining Keyshawn's displeasure with him showing up last night. And if that's the case there's definitely motive for Watson to have killed him. But he couldn't have done it himself because Collins said he was there around the time of the slaying."

Chan felt like she wanted to puke.

"So what do you think about all of this, Chan?"

All of them were looking at her and just as she was about to concur with their theory it came up. She threw up all over the file in her lap and some even got on the table. Everybody rose to their feet and Daley was on his way over to assist her.

"No," Bender said. "Go and get Morgan. Tell her to bring some wet towels. Are you okay, Chan?"

Collins just stood in place looking at the mess. She was completely embarrassed.

"I'm sorry, sir," she said, wiping her mouth.

"No, it's okay, but maybe you should consider seeing a doctor today. As a matter of fact, I'll call the one in the building," he said, reaching for the phone.

"No, sir, really it's okay. I'll be fine," Li had her own doctor and after this meeting she planned on making an appointment. The last thing she needed was for a doctor to come up there, everybody on the floor would be in her business.

Daley and Morgan made it back with wet towels and Morgan helped her get cleaned up.

"Okay everyone, we'll call an end to this meeting." Bender said stacking some papers together on the table. "No one is to share any information with the MPD until I've given the ok. We don't want them interfering with our investigations. As far as New Orleans goes, if our theory is correct, then the culprit in Ms. Madison's murder is already dead, so it doesn't matter when we decide to relinquish our findings to NOPD. Bottom line people, we've still got time solidify our cases on these three characters. We'll meet again later this week and if any significant new developments arise be sure to let me know." He was on his way out the door.

"Chan, we'll be pulling you out soon, but in the meantime, see if you can get anything concrete on why the hell that happened to that guy last night, and for Pete's sake...go see a doctor, you look pale."

* * * * *

When she made it back to the house Key was there alone. She came right in and laid on the cough. And after a few minutes, she was up rushing to the bathroom to vomit again. She was sitting on the floor nearly hugging the toilet bowl when he came in.

"What's wrong with you, girl?" Key was looking down at her with his arms stretched out touching both sides of the door frame.

"I don't know."

"This the second day I've seen you doing this, you ain't pregnant or no shit like that are you?"

She looked up. "Of course not!" Even though she'd never been pregnant and didn't know the symptoms she totally ruled it out. But reality slapped her in the face when she made the last comment. She began to think that it was a possibility.

They were in the restroom on the first level near the rear of the house which made it difficult to hear her come in. Key was talking when she closed the door.

"You don't know for sure. We didn't use protection. Are you on birth control?"

"No, I'm not; but, baby...I'm telling you I'm not pregnant."

Paris couldn't believe what she was hearing. "That dirty muthafucka'! He ain't got time for me, but he fucks this bitch and gets her pregnant! So that's why she hasn't been feeling well these last few of days." Her mind was racing with anger and jealousy when she thought about him breaking her finger she could of exploded right there.

But she'd learned from the last incident to remain cool. Instead, she made some noise in the kitchen so that they knew she was there.

Key came walking to the direction where he heard the noise. "I didn't hear you come in. How long you been here?" he had a curious look on his face.

"Not long, actually I just walked in the door, you here alone?"

She walked over and kissed him on the cheek.

"Nawh, Kimmie's in the back."

He knew that Paris had to have walked in long before she said she did and he suspected that she'd heard them by the way she was acting. But he didn't have to answer to her, so it didn't matter.

Kimmie came to the living room dabbing her face with a cold towel.

"You okay, girl?" Paris said, trying to appear concerned.

"I don't know, but I'm on my way to Urgent Care, I can't wait on no doctor's appointment. Daddy, I'll be back." "You want me to drive you? You don't look too good."

"No, I'm cool, I'll be back."

"I bet you are bitch, you don't want me there when you hear the news, huh?" she said to herself as she laid down on the couch.

* * * * *

Key chalked up the pool stick while he went over the situation with Kimmie over in his head. Hoping that she wasn't pregnant he cursed himself as he rammed the nine ball in the pocket.

The news had been reporting Smoove's massacre continuously all day. He was tired of looking at it, so when the story flashed again he quickly changed the channel and presumed practicing his shot.

The answer was simple; if she was indeed pregnant, he'd just have to get rid of it. That was surely not his intentions and he had way too much work ahead of him before he could allow one of his hoes to have a baby.

Paris came out of the room in a hurry. She was out the door before he could say a word. He called her cell phone.

"Yes, daddy?"

"Where you going?"

"To get your clothes from the cleaners, then I have two appointments lined up shortly after," she said, partly lying. She learned a valuable lesson the last time they clashed, so instead of playing with fire her new method was to continue playing her role.

Key sensed a lie but blew it off; he didn't have time to investigate every detail of the girl's whereabouts, there were more important matters at hand.

"Okay, make sure you come right back. I wanna wear one of those shirts you picking up," he had a few tricks of his own. The way she left out he knew that she had an attitude and why.

Shortly after they hung up, T.A. called him asking if he could come by his place to address an urgent matter.

"And Key, I think you should ride in one of your lowkey joints if you can."

He knew what that meant; some kind of static had arisen. And more than likely it was from the Smoove affair.

Driving one of the cars he'd purchased for the girls, Key didn't notice the agents parked on the corner as he went into T.A.'s building. Bender wanted the wiretaps covered in real-time after last night's event. Agents Collins and Daley watched the building, deciding what to do next.

"Damn, I wish we could hear their conversation," Daley said, looking through a pair of binoculars.

"What the hell am I doing with these?" he said, tossing them in the backseat. "Hell, we almost know for certain that they were involved in that guy's murder some kind of way, either that or this is one heck of a coincidence."

Collins just sat there wishing he'd shut up. Daley was constantly going over things they'd previously discussed. But he remembered that Daley was still a little wet behind the ears as he once was.

T.A was doing sit-ups as he conveyed everything to Key that his ears were hearing on the street.

"They've been riding through Atkinson all day, asking any and everybody questions about us. This lil' bitch that stays on fourteenth told me that they even offered her money if she could tell them where we was. The two niggas who she described don't sound familiar, but I know for a fact the one who Nip mentioned was his younger brother Profit."

"Profit, why does that name sound familiar? Do I know him?" he said trying to remember.

"I don't know you may, like I said he's a young nigga. Thinks he's a pimp; you know tryna' copy his older brothers."

"How many brothers did this dude have?"

"Just three that I know of, including that one."

"I'm trying to figure out what made them come snooping around over there. There was no trail leading to us unless…."

"Nawh, you know my people thorough Key. Ain't no telling maybe he told them he was coming up there yesterday and if they knew anything about the situation with him being suspected for killing yo' people; which I'm sure they probably did; then the rest don't take a rocket scientist to put together, homie."

"Okay, so what do you know about these niggas, T?"

"As much as I knew about him, which was enough to know that after that scene last night, killing him was gonna be inevitable. See he purposely came over there to fill you out; he wanted to see if you had a beef with him so he could know what his next move would be. And that's pretty much how the other two are. Fox is maybe a year or two older than me and Blake is somewhere around Smoove's age. Both of 'em get down, I don't know about Profit but shit he jumped in the water so I'm assuming he's ready for whatever too."

"Okay,' well lets smash these dudes and get this shit over with then, cause I'm not about to have no nigga out here looking for me, T."

"I'm with you, but just lay for a minute. It's too hot right now. And who knows they may just be trying to talk with us to see if we know anything. I mean with him being at the club and all right before it happened. And besides, there's nothing anybody has that can prove we had a hand in it. Just be cool and keep yo' eyes and ears open. Personally, I can't see these dudes making no fast moves; they know it's not gone end there."

This time T.A.'s assumptions were wrong. He was doing his best not to jump the gun because he knew that things could get really nasty. But what he failed to see was that the damage had already been done.

Chapter 20

When Li left the hospital building, she sat in the car crying for a while before she left the parking spot. The doctor confirmed her greatest fear. And as she looked at the document containing the babies due date it felt as though her whole world had come crumbling down. Her job, reputation, and possibly her freedom were all in jeopardy if anyone at the bureau were to find out who impregnated her. She wanted to call her mom, but was too ashamed. Ki Chan would no doubt curse her for getting pregnant outside of marriage and would probably disown her when she found out that the father was the very man whom she was put undercover to investigate and send to federal prison. She never imagined her life could take this kind of turn.

After she mustered up the strength to drive away she told herself that this would not break her. Abortion wasn't an option; Li had been a pro-lifer throughout high school and college. She was once even the president of an antiabortion group; S.A.A. - Students Against Abortion - and took pride in her commitment to the cause. She decided that she would tell no one. If she had to be a single mother so be it, the baby would have a chance at life just as she had been given.

Key called her asking about the results. She had been gone for almost three hours and hadn't made any attempts to phone him with any information.

"So, what they say?"

She closed her eyes in anguish before answering his question. A part of Chan wanted to be truthful with him, but she knew that she couldn't.

"They ran a pregnancy test and it came back negative, the doctor says it just the flu."

Just using the word pregnancy gave her the chills.

"Alright, I guess I'll see you in a minute then. You good?" Key said, elated by the news.

"Yeah, I'm okay."

But she wasn't, after they hung-up tears began to run down her face. This was supposed to be a special moment in her life, filled with excitement and happiness. That was the way Li had always envisioned being when she had her first child. But it was indeed the total opposite, she was devastated. * * * * *

When Paris took off she was steaming and tired of what she felt was a constant case of neglect. Now she was hearing that not only was he giving himself to Kimmie, but she was pregnant as well. Her emotions had the absolute best of her and whenever she got that way she always seemed to act out of impulse. Feeling compelled to take some course of action she called Profit and began to plead her case in hopes of getting the comfort she was seeking. But had she known about the current crisis between the two men she would have never contacted him, let alone agree to a brief meeting.

On the way to Profit's place, she was a little nervous, looking at every car she pasted along the way hoping not to be seen. The dry cleaner was on the other side of town and if Key got wind of the direction she was headed in she would have no way of explaining it to him.

When Paris pulled up to his house Profit couldn't believe his eyes. He didn't think she'd show. Answering the door, he wore a pleasant smile that eased her nerves. She had the look of a slut at the doctor's office awaiting H.I.V. test results.

Paris made an attempt to hug him, but when he rejected her, she suddenly began to think that maybe she'd made a mistake.

"You can have a seat," he said calmly.

When they sat down it was difficult for him to look at her. Here was the woman who left him for the nigga who happened to be at the center of his brother's murder. He wanted to kill the bitch right in the chair that she sat in. Not only for the humiliation of leaving him and taking the only other hoe that he had, but mostly for Smoove.

But Blake and Fox were there when she called him and they wanted to seize the beautiful opportunity that was before them.

She began explaining herself immediately. "I'm sorry about that day at the club. But you shouldn't have grabbed me like that. I know I was wrong for leaving you, I guess, but..." she stopped herself from saying something stupid.

"You guess, but...What's that supposed to mean?" he almost called her a bitch but realized now wasn't the time. "You know what, baby? None of that shit matters, you did what you did, I wish you hadn't, but I stopped dwelling on it the last time I saw you."

She knew Profit didn't mean what he was saying, and wondered why he had such a sudden change in demeanor. "Look, I made a mistake; I don't think I want to be with him anymore. But if we get back together things will have to be different."

"Really, how so?"

"Well, for starters I'm not working on no bullshit tracks I'm worth more than that, Profit."

He stared at her for a second. She'd just dealt a severe blow to his ego and disrespected his pimping all in one sentence. He couldn't believe she was coming to him making demands, talking drag about what she was worth. It made him feel like a complete peon.

"You got it, baby" he said. The response of not a pimp, but a true sucka. However, it was one that he felt was necessary, he had a mission to finish and if it meant biting his tongue for a minute then he would. But later, she would pay; he promised himself that much.

They talked for a while longer before her phone began to ring.

"Oh shit, hold on, baby...this him. Hey, daddy," she said, putting on her best performance. As she talked his attention was focused on the new person before him. When Paris left, she dressed like a cheap tramp. He would take her to one star low rate clothing stores, her favorite one was Rainbow and to her it was the equivalent of Macy's. Now here she was dressed from head to toe in Chanel and Fendi. He could only imagine the type of figures she had to be putting up for a nigga to take her from that to this. The thought of it made him feel even more incompetent.

When she finished the call, Paris was back on her feet. "I gotta go. I'll call you later on, we need to talk some more."

He walked her to the door. "Is this your number, the one you called me from?"

"Yeah, but please don't call it back, okay?! I might be around him or one of them other bitches and I know they'll definitely snitch on me. I'ma call you."

She left with Fox following her every move. And when she drove into the townhouse complex he noticed Key's Benz parked next to the garage. So he knew this is where he had to be living.

* * * * *

Her mood was cheery when she got inside. As Paris prepared for the client she was about to meet, she couldn't stop thinking of Profit. She was sure that things would be different and they would live better. Having access to most of Key's high-end clientele she planned to take them with her when she left. Profit would have no choice but to appreciate her now, she'd be the best he ever had. Convinced that he cared about her, she planned to make Profit a bigger and better pimp than Key could ever dream of being.

Key was coming in from his meeting with T.A. as Paris was leaving for her appointment

"Your clothes are all hanging in the closet baby, I'll see you later."

Closing the door, he couldn't help but think of how hot and cold she was today. He brushed it off and went to his closet to decide what he'd wear later on that night.

* * * * *

Security was thick that night at the club; there were armed guards at the front door, inside and patrolling the entire area. There was a crowd of hounds around the stage in the Gold room. Two females had discarded most of their clothing and were grinding on each other. High on X and Grey Goose they didn't realize the frenzy they'd caused.

When Key came in he immediately noticed what was going on and had them ushered off to the lady's room, demanding that they either put their clothes on or leave. He went into the VIP to find Red and T.A. talking amongst themselves behind the bar. Bone was at the pool table hosting a dice game at a hundred dollar a shot and a hundred on the point. He placed a few bets on Bone, who was hitting ever point he caught. Key raked in a quick thousand and was ready to walk away.

"I know you ain't done man, these dude's sweet. Ain't that right, ya'll? Bone said to the other gamblers. He laughed a little.

"Aye, Key, send me a bottle on these cats," he said, handing him two hundred-dollar bills. When he came back and handed him the champagne, Bone whispered in his ear.

"Did T.A. tell you what we talked about?"

"No."

"I seen two dudes, white and black, parked across the street when I came in. The white boy was looking through some binoculars."

"When was this and what were they in?"

"About forty-five minutes or so ago, they were in blue Impala. I don't know what they were looking for, but I know the police when I see 'em, homie."

"Alright, thanks, Bone."

"No problem, we gotta watch each other's backs. That's all I was doing."

"Aye, you gone shot the dice or what man?" a voice said from the other end of the table.

"Yeah, relax you gone get a chance to lose yo' money tonight, man, trust me," Bone said pouring himself a glass.

When Key made it over to Red and T.A. he asked him if they had anybody checking to see if the two cops were still lurking outside.

"Nawh, man, you know how them fags are. They hate to see niggas with their own shit. Probably just bored and wanna look at the bitches in line," T.A said, laughing while sipping on a drink.

"I hear you but binoculars though, that shit sounds deeper than two cops just being bored."

"You gotta relax, my man, we running a perfectly legitimate business here and whatever they on they can kiss my ass, we clean nigga. And you know what I think we need to toast to that," he grabbed a glass and poured Key up some Remy. "I know you can toss one up with us one time, baby. We just did a big thang opening up this joint. Yesterday, we were so busy with everything I forgot to take the time out to thank you two niggas. For not only trusting me ya'll bread, cause that was a lot of money to put in a nigga hands not knowing for sure when you might see a profit off it. But most importantly, I wanna thank ya'll for being one hundred with me all these years. Never once have ya'll ever been shiesty toward me and I love you niggas for that shit, lil homies."

They all slapped glasses. Key's chest was burning from the liquor.

Red and T.A. began to laugh T.A. patted him on the back. "You alright man," he said smiling.

"Yeah, I'm good."

"I'm serious about what I said though. It's rare to find real friends out here and I'm grateful to have both of y'all, niggas."

"Alright, nigga, in a minute we gone be hugging in shit over here dawg," Red said laughing.

"I ain't got no problem with that, I'm all man pimp," he said, kissing them both on the cheek. T.A. started to laugh as they frowned up

"Say, man, you need to put that Remy down, dawg," Red said, looking around, hoping no one saw it.

"Haha, man, I did that to fuck with you dudes. And what you looking around for nigga, muthafuckas in here wish they could fill our shoes. Shit, I if you go ask any bitch in here who she'd prefer being with out of all these niggas in this whole joint. I'm willing to bet cash she point in this corner. It's called money, power, and respect my niggas. And all those three words spell out is

MAN, don't ever forget that. It's the qualities that will make you irresistible to any woman."

"I can dig it, but aye, fam, where you be coming up with all those quotes in shit man?" Red asked him.

"Life, living, watching, and listening. Let me ask you this, does any of that shit be making sense?"

"Awh, yeah, plenty."

"Well, there you have it. You wanna hear something funny? I was spitting some izum to one of my hoes the other day, I really had her ears open too, man. But anyway, when I was done lacing, the bitch asked me how I got to be so smart. I said, 'Hoe, cause the game god is my daddy." Red and Key began to laugh.

"Man, get yo' ass outta here," Key said.

"On a real note though, you niggas make sure y'all keep them burners close just in case them dudes try something cute," T.A. said.

"Definitely," Red responded, putting his glass down.

"I think I need to make a few rounds, I'll catch y'all in a minute," T.A said walking toward the front.

They talked for a short while longer, and then Key decided that he wanted to rejoin Bone, who was still at the pool table, thousands of dollars ahead by now. He had so much money piled up in front of him half of the rooms were around the table watching as if it was a championship game of some sort. And when Key made it over he immediately regretted leaving.

"Damn, nigga, you got 'em in the rear heavily I see."

"I told you to stick around. I think I'm gone get up tomorrow and but myself a new toy on these clowns pimp buddy" he said brushing his hands through the stacks in front of him. Key took a quick glance and estimated it was at least thirty racks or better. The table was packed with players' young and old, eager to get their chance at Bone's winnings. Even some of the ones who'd already lost to him were still in the game. Many players had left and come back with more money, while others sent or called to have more brought up there. To avoid the any of them from being robbed security was escorting anyone to their cars who hadn't parked valet near the entrance.

This time Key stayed at the table with Bone and a couple of hours later the game was settling down and he was twenty-three thousand dollars richer. The club had been closed for some time now; Red and T.A. were in the office finishing the count on the night's proceeds.

"I see y'all did well," Red said, looking at the bag of cash Key placed on the table.

"Shit, Bone, hit 'em even harder, he had to be up around fifty Gs. Just then Bone walked in. he tossed Red and T.A.

twenty-five hundred dollars each.

"What's this?" T.A. said.

"That's for letting me work those marks, cuz."

"Yep, next time the house gotta have a cut on that big bag," he said jokingly.

"Well, I gotta get out of here, it's been fun."

"Yeah, it's past four I need to get going myself," Key said looking at the clock on the wall. He waited around talking to them until they were finished locking the place up.

When Red came out he noticed that Key's back passenger tired was on a flat. He got Key's attention and pointed to the tire.

"How the hell this happen?" he said.

"Ain't no telling, you want me to drop you off? Cause I know you not about to be out here fucking with that tire this late. Key locked up the Benz and jumped in with Red.

Chapter 21

When they arrived to Key's house there wasn't a single soul on the street. The area was quiet around that time of day, as most of the neighborhoods outside of the inner city were.

As Key was getting out of the car to go inside they noticed a dark blue taxi-cab turn onto the block off of the main street. Thinking nothing of it he walked toward the parking lot. Before he could get two feet away from the car, shots were ringing out behind him. Instantly grabbing the heat from his waist, he attempted to turn around and caught a bullet in the left arm. The impact from the shot caused him to seek cover.

He ran toward a nearby vehicle and hid behind the left side of the trunk. Looking over it, he could see that the gunman had gotten out of the cab and were coming toward him still, firing shots from the high-caliber machine gun he operated.

Thinking that he had to slow him down, Key reached over the trunk and began firing back with the thirty-two shot 40 caliber. He could hear the gunman running back and getting into the vehicle. He stood up and ran toward them blasting several rounds into the cab as the driver franticly drove away.

His arm was completely covered in blood but the adrenaline was pumping so heavily through his body he hadn't even noticed.

Red hadn't moved the silver S600 Benz no further that an inch before he was struck twice in the side of his head. And when Key got to the car he knew right away that he was dead. His body was still upright with the head hanging slightly to the side dripping blood.

Knowing the police would be on their way soon he called inside to have the girls take his money in the house. The entire house was awake, along with the neighbors who were starting to look out of their windows now.

Venus ran outside and nearly panicked when she saw all the blood that covered his shirt.

"Take this and go in the house, turn the lights out, lock the door, and no matter what…don't open it," he said handing her the bag. Venus did as he instructed, and was able to get back inside before the crowd started to form.

When the ambulance and police arrived Key was sitting on the curb. He put the gun in the backseat of Red's car to avoid the police from drawing down on him. They were asking him a million questions one after the other. He admitted to having the gun and told them that he had shot back out of fear for his life.

"So, who were the other guys?" a veteran officer asked him as he sat in the back of the ambulance with his good arm cuffed to the bed.

"I don't know."

"Bullshit, I don't believe you," the fat cop shot back. "I want to interview him at the jail as soon as he leaves the hospital," he said to the rookie officer. The officer got in the ambulance with Key and a medic who closed the doors and signaled the guy in front to take off.

When they rode past Red's Benz the pain hit him in his chest as he began to mourn the loss of his best friend. He wasn't the least bit worried about what was going to happen to him. Red had suffered the ultimate sacrifice and as he cried, he had wished he could have gotten the ups on the cab when it turned the corner. Key would forever blame himself for allowing them to get caught slipping in such a way.

Replaying the drama in his mind, he kept telling himself that he shouldn't have walked away until the cab had passed.

* * * * *

The girls were in the upstairs bedroom with the lights on watching when the morgue came to pick up Red's body. There wasn't a dry eye in the house after they zipped the bag up and wheeled him away. Everyone asked Venus if Key had been shot or was it Red's blood on his shirt, but she wasn't sure. All she could tell them was what they already knew; he was up and moving around when the police came.

Li was worried to death. When they heard the shots she was the first one at the window and knew that if was Key when she saw Red's car outside the buildings. As she kept hearing the gun shots she kept praying that he was alive. Thinking of her child, it was only natural that she was concerned about the father.

Paris felt like shit, her and Chrissy got into a heated argument earlier when she secretly confided in her confessing that she had plans to leave Key's stable and go back to Profit. Her original goal was to try and get Chrissy to join her. But after she denounced Profit, saying that he was nowhere near the man that Key was, nor could he match him mentally, Paris realized that her efforts were in vain. Nevertheless, Chrissy was still her friend; perhaps the only true one out of all the girls, so she promised that she wouldn't reveal her plot to anyone after making one last attempt to get Paris to change her mind.

She sat on the bed thinking of Key and how he must've been feeling knowing that his friend was dead. All the negative thoughts that she'd harbored inside about him had diminished and seemed to be irrelevant now. The only thing that came to mind was all the good things he'd done for her and the knowledge she'd been blessed with acquiring in the time that she'd been with him. "What was I thinking about, trying to leave him?" she thought. And after those words had sunken in, she suddenly started to feel like a traitor. *I can't leave him*, was her next thought, *I'm not calling Profit back, and I'll think of a reason to get my number changed so he can't contact me.* But little did she know, her reckless thinking and impulsive actions had just cost one person his life and had her man, not thinking he would've joined Red in his demise.

* * * * *

The bullet had gone in and out, and once the doctors examined his arm a nurse administered a tetanus shot and gave him an antibiotic to help ward off the any infections. The police then transported him to their first district station downtown. They were waiting for the medical examiner to extract the bullets from Red's skull so they could compare the tracings to the gun that Key was shooting. They'd recovered several rounds and casings so they knew that three different guns were fire. When they interviewed Key, he admitted again to his role in the incident and argued that he was acting in self defense. Wisconsin didn't have an actual law on the books for such a claim, but in this case, they didn't even have a victim. Officers confirmed that what he'd told them about his car being on a flat was the truth after they dispatched a squad to the club and found it in the parking lot. So after six hours of interrogations with various detectives asking him the same questions just in different ways, they all were inclined to believe that he was telling the truth.

They did, however, file charges for carrying a concealed weapon; which was a misdemeanor; and receiving stolen property; a felony count; for a platinum Cartier watch that he was wearing. When they inventoried his property they ran the serial number on the back of the time piece and found that it was reported stolen three months prior. The complaint also entailed a felony reckless endangerment charge because of his admittance to firing a gun in public. And he was being held without bail until the prosecutor had a chance to review the complaint.

* * * * *

Early Monday morning, Agent Chan got a call from the bureau, one that she'd anticipated, so when it came she was already dressed and ready to go. When she arrived Bender was on a conference call with the assistant D.A. handling Key's case and a high-ranking police captain who was calling on behalf of the Chief himself. She walked in and he motioned her to have a seat in one of the chairs.

"I just don't understand why you guys didn't inform us on this war that seems to have been going on amongst them," the captain said.

"At the time, we weren't sure what was actually going on, and we're in the middle of a very important investigation so we couldn't afford any leaks."

"Well, agent...thanks to you, we now have two homicides when it possibly could've only been one. This may not be of any concern to your agency, but I'm sure the city of Milwaukee and those people who live in that fine neighborhood don't appreciate your actions one bit."

"Yes, yes and I'm sorry to hear that. But gentlemen, you'll have to excuse me I have an important meeting and I'm late. Mr. Mayes, as I was saying earlier we would appreciate it if you would dismiss these matters before you in regards to the subject. We're near the end of our operation and I assure you that we will have those charges read into the indictment along with a host of other charges." The D.A. agreed and the call was ended.

"My god, I've been on the phone with those people explaining this thing for over an hour. The DA's office was very cooperative but that damn captain...he's a real pain in the ass. A bunch of residents in the building where the shooting happened Saturday have been pressing the police because they experienced one little shooting in that area."

"It was bad, sir."

"Yes, I'm sure it was, but this sort of thing is nothing more than an isolated incident in this part of the city. Now they see what the blacks and other poor folks go through every day."

"Sir!"

"I'm sorry, but it's true, the middle class people in this town have been spoiled and protected for so long that they're out of touch with reality. The world isn't perfect, and this city's no exception, now they know that."

Chan could see his frustration with the morning's events so far; she started to comment on it, but chose to keep quiet.

"Anyway, what the hell happened over there, Chan. Seems to be sort of a retaliation thing wouldn't you say?"

"Yes, it definitely was. And whoever it was they sure weren't trying to miss. Fortunately for Ke...- I mean Watson," she said correcting herself. "Fortunately for him, he was armed, otherwise he'd be dead too."

"So I hear. I don't think that would have been such a bad thing. What would you say agent, I mean would you agree?"

Chan stared at him. She almost said; "hell, no" and for a second paranoia had her wondering why he was asking her a question like that. She knew the bureau had its way of finding things out.

"Never mind, you don't have to answer that. We all have the right to due process I suppose. Anyway, actually I called you here to inform you that I'd be pulling you out of there."

"Why?" she said almost involuntarily.

"Well, the case is all but wrapped up, at least that part of it is. And besides, it's getting much too dangerous. You have a problem with this?" he was giving her a weird look.

"Ah, no, sir; of course not. In fact, I've been waiting to go home and lay in my own bed again," she said lying.

"Fine, if you have anything you need to collect from his house or the decoy pad, do so today. As of tomorrow, I'm assigning you back to the field. You can continue assisting Daley and Collins until we get this thing to the U.S. Attorney's Office."

"Okay, will that be it?"

"Yes, I guess I'll see you tomorrow then, Chan," he said smiling. "Good work, agent."

"Thank you. Good day, sir," she said as she got up to leave.

Chapter 22

After Bender was off the phone with the D.A., Key was released from the city jail with no charges being filed. The jailers on duty had no idea why he was suddenly released and when he asked the supervisor in charge he couldn't tell him anything either.

"Watson, get up your being released," the guard said tapping the bars. He didn't ask any questions as he hustled to put his shoes on.

Once he retrieved his belongings from the property window he called Venus from his cell phone to pick him up.

"Hey, daddy, where you at?"

"They just let me out, come pick me up."

After they hung up she was there in less than ten minutes.

When he got in the car she was ecstatic. His first words startled her.

"Where's that bitch, Paris?"

"She went on a date about an hour ago but should be back soon. Why what's wrong, baby?"

"I don't know, but we about to find out."

Venus was the only one he would share certain information with because he knew that she was not only down with him one hundred percent. But he also knew that she was a real bitch and she understood the streets just as he did, if not better.

When they made it to the townhouse no one else was there. Venus took the bloodstained shirt off him and threw it in the trash. She made him a hot bath in the whirlpool and helped him clean up.

"So, you did get hit? Oh, baby, we were all worried sick you know. And I'm so sorry about Red."

He could barely stand the mention of his best friend since childhood; the pain of losing him was worst than all the times he was let down and eventually dumped and abandoned by his father. Venus had never seen him so vulnerable, and she wished she could do something to change what happened, but that was impossible. So she did the best that she could and that was to simple be there in any way he needed her.

"Have you been hearing that bitch talking about that nigga, Profit, that she used to be wit?" he was looking into her eyes searching for any hint of a lie.

"Hell, nawh, baby; you know if I did, I would have brought it to your attention right away."

Key knew that she was telling the truth. Venus may have been a lot of things, but being disloyal to him wasn't one of them. She wanted to ask him a few questions about where he was going with this

Paris business, but knew that there was no need because she would be answered soon enough.

When Key dried off, he went into the bedroom with the intention of getting dressed.

"Here go your pajamas. I think you need to chill out for a couple of days. At least until your arm is feeling a little better. I talked to Keysha last night; your mama wants you to call her as soon as possible."

She was straightening up the room constantly bending over to pick up things off of the floor and since Venus never wore anything around the house except for thin panties and a bra he couldn't help but notice the camel toe that kept showing up every time she bent down. Something that he looked at daily and never paid it any mind. But jail had a way of making one appreciate the simplest pleasures of life that we seemed to take for granted every day. And before she knew it, he had her on the bed drilling that pussy from the back like a sergeant. When he finished, Venus looked at him in disbelief then began laughing.

"That's what a couple days in there did to you, huh, daddy?"

They shared a quick laugh together.

"Well, anyway, thanks," she said, lying back on the bed.

He smiled. "Get yo' crazy ass outta here, girl," he said, sitting on the bed.

They talked about the night of the incident some more until he heard Paris come in.

Venus went downstairs and after he put on the pajama set he joined them. Paris was all over him as soon as he hit the stairs.

"Hey, baby, you ain't tell me daddy was hear, V?"

Venus didn't respond she just continued watching TV.

She looked at Key who was wearing a stone brick face. "What?"

"You tell me what trick. You fucking around with that sucka ass ex-pimp of yours again, bitch."

From the look that came across her face, Key knew that his hunch was right. Somebody had to tell them where he resided. He was sure of it because he and Red were checking the whole way there to make sure they didn't have a tail. They even circled the block once before finally stopping at the buildings. In the city jail, he wrecked his brain for two days trying to figure out where he'd heard the name, *Profit*. Then he remembered Paris saying his name the night after leaving the Empire Room. Before then, he never knew his name nor did he ask; it was irrelevant, he had knocked him for his hoes and that was all that mattered. Paris was dumb founded. She wondered how he knew about her seeing Profit.

"Chrissy must have said something," she said to herself,

"that bitch."

"I just talked to him once, daddy, I swear that was it." Key was surprised at how fast she confessed.

"You lying, untrustworthy, bitch! Do you realize my nigga's dead because of yo' trifling ass?"

"What, what you talking about daddy?"

She had no idea that Fox followed her home and was also trying to understand why he was implying that her actions somehow was the reason for Red's death.

"Don't give me that shit. Just go upstairs and get yo' shit. I'm canceling yo' contract. No...better yet, have a seat."

He turned to Venus who was turning up her nose at Paris.

"Go up there and gather up all her stuff and bring it down here, then you can call her nothing ass a cab."

"Daddy come on, where am I gonna go, please?" she was sobbing uncontrollably.

II don't care where you go, you lucky I'm letting you do it alive," he gritted his teeth when he said it.

Venus emerged with all of her belongs in two big bags. But when the cab arrived she attempted one last desperate plea to stay as she was walking out the door.

"Keep the money you just collected from that date and like I said, be grateful that I spared you bitch!"

He closed the door in her face and she wiped her face dragging the two bags through the parking lot.

"Where's the other three?"

"Chrissy went on an out of town call to Port Washington, she should be back tonight. Classy been busy working since nine o'clock this morning, and Kimmie had a date this morning at eight thirty; she was here when I left, I'm assuming she's busy."

"You assume, what the…" he had to catch himself, Key was still a little heated, actually he hated to let Paris go, but his love and respect for Red couldn't allow her to stay. She brought him money and jewels by the bags, but none of it weight up to what she just took away from him.

"Call her and see what's happening!"

Venus knew that he was stressed over everything that had happened thus far. The man had been shot; a friend killed, and he had to dismiss a lucrative hooker; all in less than seventy-two hours. She totally understood his frustration.

When she called Kimmie, the phone went to voice mail twice.

"She's not answering, baby; probably in the middle of a date."

"Don't worry about it," he said calmly. She walked behind the sofa and began to massage his temples.

Paris called Profit as soon as she got in the cab. She had nowhere to go and figured she may as well go back to him thinking he'd be pleased with her return.

He answered after a few rings. "Hello."

"Hey, where you at?" she said, trying to sound normal as she could.

"Why?" he was leery after what they had done and wasn't sure if she was being sent as a decoy now.

"Cause I need a place to put my things, I just left him."

She didn't want to tell him what all had just really happened. It was much too embarrassing to tell anyone. "Okay, what you calling me for?" Just like that he did a 360 on her.

"I thought we..."

"Well, you thought wrong. But you know what you can do. Lose my number."

Like Key, Profit wished he could bring Paris on board, especially now that she had stepped her game up several notches, but to mix with her any further would be the move of a greedy fool. She had served her purpose.

By now, Paris was confused with four hundred dollars to her name and everything she owed in the backseat of a cab. She had the driver take her to a hotel.

* * * * *

Chan was back at home for first time in months sitting in her favorite chair that was arranged under the hand lamp in her living room. She wanted so badly to answer the phone when Key's number appeared on her caller ID. After leaving behind Venus, she grabbed a picture of them that they took out one night in a club downtown. But what would she tell him, that she was an undercover F.B.I. agent sent to put him away? This surely wasn't the first time the thought had crossed her mind in the last month. And each time it did the seed grew even more. If one thing was for sure, it was the idea that she had to do something about the situation He was the father of her child and she felt a moral obligation to see to it that they were given a chance to have a relationship where Key could play an active role in the child's life.

But how, the bureau had mountains of incriminating evidence on him already with her and the wiretaps being the most damaging. *But what if she disappeared*, well, then there was still the phone conversations; hundreds of hours of them. Maybe she could gain access to them somehow; the recordings were all stored in an electronic database on the system at the office. She knew from previous investigations that after the wires were captured the system would automatically start the recording process. After the calls were ended it would then save them into the database giving each recording its own identification number so that they could be easily retrieved. All of these electronic files stayed in the building in their database until investigations were finalized and ready to be processed the U.S. Attorney's Office. Once the prosecutors got the case the files were then transferred to the main server of whatever regional office the case was being tried in. Madison was the head office for Wisconsin so that's where the files would go.

Chan knew that if she wanted a shot at deleting the recording she would have to do so before the case was ready for a grand jury, which meant that, she didn't have much time. Bender would be pushing hard for them to finish especially with all the recent violence erupting around the case now. She took one last scoop of the vanilla ice cream before putting it back in the freezer and heading to her room to prepare for bed. She put the picture of her and Key under the huge pillow and turned off the lamp before lying down. Closing her eyes, she thought of having a son and smiled at a vision of him and Key playing together in the park. A vision that she was determined to see, no matter how high the cost.

Chapter 23

The postal carrier always delivered the mail in the early morning hours, usually when he was sleeping. But due to the events over the past week, Key hadn't slept much and when he did, lightly was an understatement. So after he heard the parcels hit the floor in the front hall he went to collect the articles. Most of it was monthly bills and a few pieces of junk mail. But there was a small priority package that had been post marked that day originating from Milwaukee. The sender's address was simply labeled *Hello*. Once he was back in the living room, he sat the other letters on the coffee table and ripped the small envelope open the note inside read as follows: *"Hey, call me @ 414-555-1000, you know who, do so from a payphone in the Grand Avenue Mall near your house. If you use any other phone, I will not answer. I'll wait for your call today, an hour after you get this note, 11:00 a.m. sharp!!"*

Key stared at the letter wondering was this some sort of prank, who this person was, and why did they want him to call from the mall only. He toyed with the possibility of it being Kimmie since no one had heard from her in nearly four days. But didn't understand why she would be sending him a note through Priority Mail. However, once he called everyone in his immediate circle he was convinced it had to be her.

* * * * *

After parking in the structure, Key found a set of payphones near the third floor entrance doors next to a vitamin water vending machine. Scanning the area he hadn't noticed anyone who looked out of place. The mall had just opened its doors to shoppers so the traffic on that Thursday was thin. It was exactly 11:01 a.m. when he placed the call. His eyes jotted around as he waited for an answer with his back turned to the phone.

"Hey."

It was her.

"What's the deal with all this," he said. His nerves were slightly calming now that he knew for sure who it was.

The moment of truth had come and Li was more nervous now than she'd been the other day when she concocted her plan to tell him the truth. Once she crossed that line and revealed herself to him. Life as she knew it would be no more, but her final thought was that it had to be done.

"There are a lot of things that I need to tell you and I really don't know what's about to happen, baby; but I love you, and I just want you to know that I'm following my heart."

Her palms were sweating; this wasn't as easy as she'd anticipated it would be.

Key didn't know what to think because he thought that he knew everything about her that was important enough to be told to the Pope himself.

"So, what do you have to tell me?"

"I want us to talk face to face. Get in your car and drive straight up Wisconsin Avenue until you get to Fredoradt Memorial Hospital. I'll meet you in the small cafeteria on the lower level. I'll be watching, so there'll be no need to call notifying me of your arrival."

"Why didn't you just say all this in yo' lil note?" he was curious, Kimmie sounded and talked like a totally different person than the one he'd known.

"I wasn't sure if the letter would end up in your hands, I couldn't take any chances. I know you must have a lot of questions and I promise I'll answer them all when I see you."

"Fair enough, baby. I'll be there," he said before ending the call.

When he got back in the car, Key placed the 9mm under the seat of the rental car. Key was taking no chances with his life, after what happened to Red, he vowed to never leave home without it. He didn't even like staying at his place anymore and had Venus searching for a new domain, some place on the outskirts of Milwaukee where it wouldn't be as easy to find him.

Driving up Wisconsin Avenue, he wondered where Kimmie was, it was obvious that she'd been tracking his every move. *Why was she so paranoid?* All that talk about him possibly being followed had Key looking at every car that was near him. *And by who?* was the question he wanted to ask her. He'd thought of a dozen things that she had to tell him. But her being a federal agent was the furthest thing from his mind.

When he made the right turn on to the hospital grounds, Chan was certain they didn't have a tail on him. Even though she knew Daley and Collins whereabouts at the time, Bender may have had others involved that she wasn't aware of, not to mention M.P.D. Only fools rush in, and she knew better than to move without having a solid plan in place.

She drove past the parking lot and seen that the gold Pontiac Grand Prix Key that he drove there in was parked and empty. And after parking on the other side of the building, she made her way through the emergency room sliding doors. The signs on the walls lead her to a set of elevators that would take her to the lower level.

Key was in the cafeteria drinking from a bottle of apple juice while he pretended to read the latest issue of *Time*. There was a row of windows in the hallway just outside and as he looked up she motioned for him to meet her down the hall.

What the hell, she acting like the government is watching us or something, he thought as he got up from the tiny couch.

When he made it to the hallway, Li was standing in the doorway of a small waiting room area just down the hall.

When Key entered the room, she embraced and kissed him on the cheek.

"How's your arm?" she said, looking at the sling.

"It's okay. So talk to me, what's going on?"

She smiled at him and as they sat down, began to tell him everything.

* * * * *

Sidney Bender received the call that afternoon from his boss in Madison. Anne Hennings had talked with both the Mayor and Chief of Police; they were stressing their concerns about Bender and his lack of communication with the M.P.D. Her position was the same as Benders so she didn't hear their cries too well. But she didn't need them contacting Washington either and after Bender gave her a quick briefing on the cases she ordered a closing on the matters to be within a week in an effort to ward off any future pressure that could come down in the near future from D.C.

MOTIVATION: MASTERING THE GAME

* * * * *

Key didn't know what to think once she finished telling him who she really was and why she was there. What he couldn't figure out was why Li had come clean with him; surely she didn't want to go from being a F.B.I. agent to a prostitute/thief. Chan had yet to tell him about what would probably be the biggest shocker next to her being an agent for the Government.

He sat in the chair playing with the few whiskers that had recently grown on his young chin.

"So, now what? You told me about the case they have against me and my partna' T.A., seems like we on our way to the pen. Which brings me to ask you why'd you even bother telling me in the first place?"

"I'm telling you because I'm pregnant and you're the father."

"You what?" he was leaning on the edge of his chair now.

"I said, I'm pregnant, and besides that, I think you're a good person in spite of what you do. It's not like you're forcing those girls to do the things that they do for you. It's the way you live. I feel crazy saying this, but I've actually grown to respect you for what you do. I love you and I want to be a part of your world."

Key was still looking at her stunned by all that she'd just told him, especially her pregnancy. It was as though she'd dealt him death in one hand and new found hope in the other.

"So, tell me...how do I get out of this mess, baby? Cause I haven't the slightest clue."

"Well, first of all I don't know if we can get this to go away altogether. There are a few elements to the case that are pretty open and shut, but my concern is to do away with the heavier charges so that we can get you a lighter sentence if they get a conviction."

Then she went on giving him the details to the plan she'd devised to turn the situation around.

"You think that shit's gonna work?" he said, clinging to the idea of avoiding prison.

"It should, you just need to see to it that when the U.S. Attorney summons those girls to appear before a grand jury that they don't say that you're their pimp. Even without the phone conversations they still have a strong case if those girls cooperate."

"Why can't I just have 'em disappear?"

"That won't do anything, baby this is the government; they'll hold the case; send Marshals to find them; and drag them into court. And believe me...they'll track them down with no problem. You're just gonna have to prep them really well before they go into that courtroom."

"How much time do we have?"

"Not long, I'd say a few weeks until the case is officially wrapped up. Then they'll issue subpoenas for them once the D.A. gets a date to present his case before the grand jury."

Before they finished their meeting and parted ways, Key expressed his concerns for T.A. She admired his loyalty to his friend and assured him that she'd do everything in her power to see to it that they both stayed free.

While walking through the long corridor, all he thought about was dodging a lengthy sentence in federal prison. The initial shock from what he'd just heard had worn off and his mind was in survival mode.

Based on everything shared with him, Key knew she wouldn't be backing out on him. The pregnancy and information she'd given him alone was enough to ensure that their investigation had been extremely compromised. So, if all else failed, that would surely be his trump card against the government.

Key wondered what the D.A. would say when he found out that he'd managed to flip the very agent who they sent to take him down. No doubt about it, he had an arsenal to defend himself in court, and the baby would be his strongest weapon of all.

* * * * *

When he emerged from the hospital doors wearing the crimson-colored silk Gucci shirt, it was impossible for Agent Daley not to notice him.

He'd watched Chan leave just minutes prior in the agency's sedan and ruled out their presence at the hospital at the same time as being coincidental. The only question was, what were they up to?

To be continued...

To learn more about **SWIFT**
visit www.swiftnovels.com

MOTIVATION

PT.2 "THE CHASE"

A NOVEL BY SWIFT

RH PUBLISHING PRESENTS
A NOVEL BY
SWIFT
MOTIVATION
3
"THE EXIT"
BREAKING NEWS
IN MILWAUKEE
5:08
83°
TODAY'S
TMJ 4
HD

RH PUBLISHING PRESENTS

STAR STRUCK

A NOVEL BY SWIFT

ORDER FORM

Motivation
Book Series

-BARGAINS RATES -
PURCHASE ANY 2 BOOKS FOR ONLY $20.00
PURCHASE THE ENTIRE MOTIVATION BOOK
SERIES FOR ONLY $28.00!!

Quantity	Book Title	Cost	Total
	MOTIVATION MASTERING THE GAME	$11.99	
	MOTIVATION II THE CHASE	$12.99	
	MOTIVATION III THE EXIT	$14.99	
	VIA U.S. PRIORITY MAIL S/H $2.99 FIRST BOOK $1.00 EA ADDITIONAL BOOK WISCONSIN RESIDIENTS MUST ADD 5.6% SALES TAX		
	Total Submitted		

MAKE CHECK & MONEY ORDERS PAYABLE TO:
R.H. PUBLISHING, LLC P.O. BOX 11642 MILWAUKEE, WI 53211

Name_____

ID#_____

Institution Name_____

Address_____

City_____ State _____ Zip _____

FOR ONLINE ORDERS VISIT:
www.swiftnovels.com

Made in USA - Kendallville, IN
1221421_9780615834696
01.04.2021 1053